FAIRHOPE MARREN

FAIRHOPE MARREN

©2019 Painted Life Publishing LLC

All rights reserved.

TABLE OF CONTENTS

Chapter 1 1

Chapter 2 13

Chapter 3 29

Chapter 4 36

Chapter 5 41

Chapter 6 50

Chapter 7 54

Chapter 8 67

Chapter 9 81

Chapter 10 91

Chapter 11 106

Chapter 12 109

Chapter 13 122

Chapter 14 134

Chapter 15 138

Chapter 16 152

Chapter 17 160

Chapter 18 164

Chapter 19 168

Chapter 20 180

Chapter 21 191

Chapter 22 199

CHAPTER 1

"Hi Baby, how was your flight?"

Alec Jacobs stood at the gate watching his love exit the plane.

A perk of being a DC detective, he went through security without issue. Marren leaped into Alec's arms. She tangled herself around him, dropping her carry on at his feet. Her face dove into her favorite place, the nape of his neck. She inhaled, breathing him in, and everything felt right again.

"Just fine." Her southern accent was charming and so very sexy to his ears. "I missed you."

Her lips touched his skin and he squeezed her that much tighter.

"I missed you." Alec ran his hand from the crown of her head to her lower back. His hand returned to the nape of her neck. "Give me those lips." His kiss was far from gentle. It claimed her as his and it only ended when he had tasted enough to make it to his car.

Alec picked up her carry on asking, "Weekend ritual or something new?"

"Ritual is fine. I'm starving. I ran late from work and barely made my plane. I didn't have time for dinner before I boarded. Then the pilot asked to talk to me, which was surprising and time consuming so no snacks either. I've flown on his route several times." Marren had been with the FBI for nearly eight years, recruited out of graduate school.

Alec's hand slipped from her lower back when they walked single file through a crowd.

He leaned forward saying, "I'm sure that has more to do with how beautiful you are and not that you're carrying a gun. I would ask to speak to you too." He chuckled.

"Very Funny. But you're right. He never mentioned my weapon. Just asked if this was a business or pleasure trip."

The corner of Alec's mouth lifted, "What did you tell him?"

"Pleasure." Marren bounced her eyebrows. "That was the wrong thing to say because that opened the door to an offering of drinks. His home base is DC."

Alec nodded. He wasn't surprised. Marren Quinn turned heads. She was beautiful, putting it mildly. He looked her over for just a moment before focusing on maneuvering them out of the airport. The Friday evening flights were always packed, and the corridors were jammed full of commuters. Marren's body was to be worshipped, part of their week-end ritual, and the sooner he could get them out of the airport, the better. He couldn't wait to get his hands on her beautiful full breasts, thin waist, round, firm ass and toned legs that went on for miles. He thought to himself that she was swimsuit magazine cover worthy.

They stole a couple of quick glances as they moved through the airport, with Alec admiring her tropical ocean blue eyes that did him in every time. When Marren wanted her way and flashed him those eyes, he caved. He had learnt early on not to argue eye to eye because there would never be an argument he would win. His hand traveled to her hair, which was thick and deep dark brown – almost black – and fell to the middle of her back. It was so soft to the touch and he wound it around his hand to enjoy.

"And what did you say?" Alec asked.

Marren shrugged with a sassy grin, "I figured I would see what you had planned before making up my mind. I told him I would get back to him," she winked.

Alec dropped her hair and gave her a swat on the ass, "You better not have said that." He laughed playfully. Alec's hand wrapped around her waist, letting her know she was his.

They stopped at a local pub for a burger and beer. The pub was within walking distance to Alec's condo. He lived near Georgetown University and there were a ton of restaurants in the area, all of which they frequented on Marren's visits.

The condo was pricey and on a DC Detectives salary, it was not the norm. Alec and his sister Addison lost their parents to a fatal car accident when both siblings were in their twenties. No money in the world replaced the loss, but both Alec and Addison were taken care of financially. Alec was stationed in Afghanistan when he received the news of his parent's accident. Addison was only twenty and a sophomore in college, while Alec had joined the Army at eighteen. He had worked his way up and through college, becoming a Ranger, and one of the best. He was six years in when the accident happened and took some leave time to make sure Addie would be ok after the funeral.

The two were close. She was all he had in the world until Addison met Max. Addison was married to Max Ross, amazing chef and entrepreneur, but most importantly, a wonderful husband. His sister and brother-in-law lived in Fairhope, Alabama, which is how and where he met Marren, Addison's best friend.

"It's freezing here," Marren complained. DC was cold in early December. Fairhope's temperatures were still in the fifties and sixties.

Alec smiled and leaned in, "I'm going to warm you up. Are you finishing that beer?"

"Yes. I'm going to finish it." She took a sip. Marren wanted to talk. She had wanted to talk for months but Alec was good at distraction. "So, I was thinking about Christmas and New Year's," Marren smiled.

"I have bad news about both. I'm not going to be able to leave DC. We have too many detectives on vacation for me to get any time off. I'll be here," Alec said, genuinely disappointed.

He knew Marren was going to be upset. He figured he would just rip the band-aid off. He wasn't excited to open the door for a discussion. Alec had managed to dodge the hard questions for the last month as Marren was becoming less patient with their living situation.

Marren looked more aggravated than disappointed, "Really? You can't do one or the other? Why didn't you put in for it? You didn't have Thanksgiving off and it's been four weeks since our last weekend together.

"I had last Christmas off." Alec took a pull on his beer.

"How long have you known? It's three weeks away and you are just now telling me?"

Alec sighed, "I was hoping someone's plans would change and I could negotiate at least one of the holidays. Look, I'm not going to have any time off. You should stay in Fairhope or go see your parents, no reason for both of us to be miserable and freezing in DC. I'll take a long weekend right after the New Year and come to you."

Marren's face looked anything but happy. "Looks like you have it all worked out." She took the final sip of her beer. "Where are we headed? I mean I thought we would be together more by now, not less." She placed the empty beer mug back on the napkin.

The last thing Alec wanted to do was start the weekend out with *moving to Fairhope* dialogue. He'd heard it from his sister earlier in the week and now Marren was starting. He was definitely not going to discuss it on Friday night, setting a miserable tone for the weekend.

"We are headed to the condo so I can strip you out of your clothes and make love to you."

Alec stood and put money on the table. Moving between her legs, he wrapped his arms around her waist. He nuzzled and kissed her neck, then picking her up off the stool, he took her by the hand, walking out of the bar.

Good Lord the man was fine. The things she wanted him to do to her. Marren watched Alec pull his t-shirt off while she plugged in her phone and computer to charge. Alec's body was sculpted to perfection; six-pack abs, muscular arms and chest, and pelvic muscles that for the moment were partially hidden by his jeans. Alec turned, walking to the bathroom that was connected to the bedroom. His sexy backside, buns of steel and leg muscles galore filled out his denim. He was an advertisement for spending quality time at the gym, along with good genetics.

Alec brushed his teeth before returning to the bedroom. Marren had slipped her jeans and sweater off. She walked past him in a bra and panties, heading for the bathroom. He grabbed her from behind and wrapping his arms around her waist, he burrowed into her shoulder.

"You smell good. Look so good. Are you ready for the pleasure you told the pilot about?"

Marren giggled, "Let me brush my teeth."

She squirmed away from him, completing her walk to the bathroom. Marren opened the medicine cabinet to all of her things. Alec had surprised her on a visit almost a year ago to a stocked cabinet and shower full of every product she used, including a toothbrush with a purple handle to contrast his blue one. She smiled, remembering the gesture.

Returning to the bedroom, the lights were dim, covers were pulled down and music played. Alec knew what she liked, and it was never bright lights. She wasn't self-conscious or shy, she just liked the lighting and music low. She liked things romantic. Marren could hear Alec in the kitchen.

"Will you bring me…" She stopped talking when he walked in with a bottle of water for her.

"A bottle of water?" He smiled, handing her the bottle.

She nodded, "Thank you." Marren turned, placing it on the nightstand.

"Take those off for me," Alec instructed in the way that he always did. His voice was sexy and in charge as his eyes watched her.

Marren turned to him, "You take them off."

Alec smirked. It was going to be one of those nights. They both enjoyed his dominance in their bed, but now and then Marren wouldn't follow his instructions without some persuading. It usually stemmed from her feeling out of control out of the bedroom. Alec walked to her in his boxer briefs, sexy as all get out. Marren let her eyes wander over his body, appreciating him. Six foot three inches of all man and muscle. His boxer briefs bulged with excitement. His hand took the side of her neck with his thumb, tilting her chin up to look at him.

Alec's eyes were steamy, "You're going to be sassy?" He smiled.

Marren slightly shrugged one shoulder, "Maybe."

Alec's lips brushed over hers, "I'll spank you."

"That's not a deterrent." Marren felt her heart race.

He consumed her mouth, teeth and tongue raking her lips before his tongue dove inside, tasting her. Alec's kisses were more like love making to her mouth, leaving her winded and wanting. This kiss was used to turn her thinking around to him being in charge.

He pulled away, "Love me?"

Marren nodded.

He spun his fingers around, telling her to face away from him. She did as she was instructed. Alec unclasped her bra, letting his hands run over shoulders and down her arms, removing it. His wet, open mouth tasted her shoulder, his tongue doing a little dance across her skin. Her hair was brushed to the side so his mouth could trail to her neck.

Just below her ear he whispered, "Get on the bed, baby."

Marren lay on her side, watching Alec. He opened his nightstand, pulling out a small bottle. He opened it, pouring some of its contents in his palms. His hands rubbed together as he knelt on the bed near her thighs.

"That smells good." She smelled hints of the clean sheets and lavender.

He nodded, "I need your back."

Marren lay flat with her face turned to the side. She felt Alec straddle her upper thighs. Starting at her lower back, both hands moved up to her shoulders. The massage and his caress were heaven.

"This won't make me forget that I want to talk," Marren commented in a voice that was not fully awake.

"Mmm hmm. Not tonight. I want to hear other sounds come out of that beautiful mouth."

Alec continued to work her muscles until he felt her completely relax onto the bed. Moving to stand at the foot of the bed, his fingers took the sides of her panties and pulled them down her legs, tossing them to the floor.

Alec grinned, "I love taking off your frilly panties."

His hands worked from the bottom of her feet and up her legs to her ass cheeks that were lovely and round. Alec concentrated on each and every muscle. He listened to her breathing and loved the soft sighs and moans she made when he moved to different areas of her beautiful body.

His lips and tongue tickled the skin on her neck, "Feel good?" His massage had been thorough.

Marren was so relaxed that speaking took work, "Mmm."

Alec ran his tongue and lips on her shoulders, the little moisture that his lips provided as he exhaled warm breath causing chills. When Marren lifted slightly to turn over, Alec's body covered hers, stopping her movement. She continued to lay flat on her stomach. Alec continued caressing her with this mouth, working down her back. He loved the way her lower back curved down and back up to the top of her bottom. He kissed across the curve, moving his own body between her legs. Marren's bottom was peppered with kisses.

"You have the most beautiful ass."

Alec took her hips in his hands, encouraging her to lift off the bed. His knees spread her legs and Marren propped up on her hands and knees. Alec's hand ran up her spine to her shoulders, pushing her gently to lower her upper body back to the pillow.

He moved to the edge of the bed so he could lower his face between her legs. His tongue said hello in a long, seductive taste from her favorite spot to her opening. His hands spread her legs and hips, opening her all the more so his mouth could tickle and toy.

"Nice and ready for me. You taste delicious." Alec's fingers pressed into her, holding her tight so she couldn't move when he sucked her sensitive flesh into his mouth.

The pillow that she clenched with her fingers muffled the moan that barreled out of her. Marren was shocked in the best way; his mouth was so good at this angle, so different. Her climax was building in a fury, only seconds in his mouth and she was losing control. Her first reaction was to pull away slightly to slow the sensation, but his hands wouldn't allow it.

"Slow down," she panted, but it was too late, she was in the midst of a fast eruption that shook her body.

Marren could feel the tingles to her toes, making them curl. She knew her cries of release were loud, even muffled by the pillow. Alec's mouth, more gentle now, let the last pulses rush through her. When her body was on cloud nine, she tried to collapse to the bed, but still his hands held her in place.

"You're so sexy, fuck baby. Stay right here." He let go of her hip, fingers sliding inside her. "So wet. I love to make you come." Alec's fingers started to work their magic.

"Not yet. Not yet." Marren's voice was ragged.

Alec continued moving his fingers, pushing her to give him the reaction he wanted, "Yes. Right now. I say when, remember?"

She tightened around him and gave a gentle whimper. This time, this orgasm, he let her body fall to the bed. Alec was strong and flipped her over like she was a rag doll.

His face dove between her legs, fingers spread her apart, thigh on his shoulder, "Is this mine?" His teeth nibbled at her.

Marren's fingers threaded in his short blond hair, "Yes." Her voice was that of a sexual whimper.

Alec gave her a long lick, "When I say to take your clothes off, what do you do?" Alec's mouth vacuumed her in.

Marren came off the bed slightly, arching her back. "Alec!" she cried out. The orgasm was right there for the taking; she pulled his hair, "Oh God."

Alec's fingers slipped in again, arching in a forward motion.

He was urging her forward, "What do you do?" Alec smiled, feeling her body begin to tremble.

His fingers were taken a hold of by her body.

"I take off my clothes." Her voice broke with airy sounds.

"That's right, because I want to have my way with you. You like when I have my way don't you?" Alec's voice crooned.

Marren's body released and her head fell to the side, "Yes."

Alec kissed over her stomach, bringing his mouth to her breasts. His lips tugged at each nipple with gentle licks and kisses. Then her breast was palmed for more aggressive suckling. Marren's neck arched, pushing her head deep into the pillow, her fingers raked his scalp, pulling his hair.

His hands took hers, raising them over her head to press them to the bed. Alec lifted off her slightly and taking his cock in his hand, he lined up to enter her. He hesitated and while looking in her eyes, he teased her, rubbing the tip against the very spot his tongue had wreaked havoc upon.

Marren lazily blinked her eyes, trying to remove her hands from his hold. "I want to touch you."

"After you come." Alec breached her entrance, slowly pushing inside.

"You feel so good," Marren said before turning her face to the side.

Alec felt the same. There was nothing better than being inside Marren. His movements were slow and deep as he savored every minute. "I love being inside you. I was meant to be right here." Alec was deep, circling his hips, watching her suffer in pleasure.

Marren's hips lifted to meet him. "Harder, Alec. Make me come."

Alec kissed her neck and mouth then lifted to a kneeling position. His hands spread her knees so he could see how beautiful she was as he slammed his cock deep inside her. It wasn't long and Marren was crying his name. He lowered to kiss her with his body covering hers. Marren's hands were now free to roam; she held his lower back, dragging down to his ass cheeks. The grip and pull her hands provided set a hard and fast pace, encouraging Alec to enjoy his own release. He held out for a short time but in the end, she claimed him.

Alec was gentle as he pulled her to his chest while he lay on his back, his breathing slowing. Marren's leg was bent at the knee, covering his thigh and her cheek rested on his chest as her arm hugged across his middle. This was Marren's signature; every inch of her touched him. Both his hands found parts of her to caress and hold.

Marren lifted her face slightly, kissing his chest, "I love you, Alec."

"Me too, Baby." Alec lifted his head off the pillow, kissing the top of her head.

He continued to touch her everywhere his hands could reach. Sleep found both of them quickly.

It was nearly 2 a.m. when Marren woke to use the bathroom. She returned to the side of the bed, seeing Alec sprawled out with the sheet barely covering his pelvis. He had felt her leave and could feel her standing next to the bed. Alec opened his eyes and pushed the bed sheet away. His hand took her wrist, pulling her to him. Marren knelt on the bed only long enough to move over Alec, straddling him. His hand stood his cock up for Marren to slowly lower on to.

She took him in deep, causing her head to fall back. "You're so big, so hard."

Alec's hands held her hips tight, pulling and pushing until she was panting. He made sure she was over the edge before he shifted, rolling her off of him. Alec got up and stood at the edge of the bed. He pulled Marren's legs towards him, spreading them wide. Re-entering her, his strokes were quick, long and deep. She grabbed at his hands.

"Put your hands over your head," Alec instructed.

Marren didn't do what he said so he slowed his movements, waiting for her. When she followed his direction, his pace quickened. Alec enjoyed watching her laid out before him, her breasts bouncing with every thrust. He spent a good amount of time in this position, getting Marren's body ripe for another orgasm.

"You are so beautiful and mine." Alec pulled out of her and flipped her over. Both hands lifted her hips, pulling her back towards the edge of the bed. His cock found her entrance and slid in. "Am I too deep?" Alec asked, moving gently. This angle was sometimes tricky.

Marren's upper body remained on the bed with only her ass and hips in the air. She gripped the sheets, breathing heavy. "No. You're good." Her voice was a croak that switched to soft sounds and panting when he picked up speed and depth.

"Tell me if it's too much." Alec pounded into her.

The slapping of their skin only thrilled him all the more.

"Oh God, Alec," Marren moaned with enjoyment.

"Is it good? Come for me." Alec was on the verge of coming but he needed her to get there first.

Marren cried out into the mattress. Her body pushed back against his cock and he felt her give over to him.

He was quick to follow, "Fuck. You are so fucking tight. Christ." Alec was spent, exhausted and more than sated.

CHAPTER 2

A lec leaned against the wall at the edge of the kitchen watching Marren hum while she scrambled eggs. She wore his t-shirt from the night before.

She turned, startled, "Good morning."

"Good morning." He walked over, kissing her lips, the lips that spoke the southern dialect that his mind heard whenever he thought of her. He smiled, "Coffee?"

"Of course. Breakfast will be ready in five minutes," Marren smiled.

They had a lazy morning eating breakfast, reading the Saturday paper and showering together.

"What do you want to do today?" Marren asked as she pulled on her jeans.

"I have an idea. Dress warm." Alec pulled open the doors of his closet to select his clothes for the day.

They returned to Alec's condo after ice-skating at Washington Harbour. The rink was located near the Georgetown Waterfront and was the largest outdoor rink in DC. It was packed full of couples and families and eateries and places to sit and sip hot chocolate were plentiful. The afternoon was fun and romantic. They held hands and warmed each other with long, slow kisses that ignited a fire that needed to be put out.

"I can't remember the last time I went ice skating. Thank you for thinking of that. It was so much fun." Marren walked through the door Alec held open for her.

He grabbed her hand, pulling her close to him. "You looked good doing it. I was impressed."

"Growing up in Minneapolis, winter sports are a given. It seemed like the snow and ice went on forever. I'm so glad I moved south." She giggled, "But Fairhope needs an ice rink."

Alec enjoyed seeing her giddy from the fun they had that afternoon. He responded, "Boston was cold as a kid. I did more sledding than skating."

Alec helped her take her winter coat off and removed his. He hugged her waist while his face nuzzled in her neck.

"You are a natural on the ice. I don't think there is any sport or physical activity that you're not good at." She wrapped her arms around his neck, running her fingers through his hair.

Alec turned them, placing Marren's back against his closed front door.

"There is this physical activity that I would like to practice a little more to make sure I have it."

His hand slid underneath her sweater, feeling the soft, smooth skin of her waist. Fingers trailing up and around her back unclasped her bra so he could skim underneath, cupping her breast. His thumb danced across her nipple that was at attention.

Marren's mouth touched his neck, "You have this."

Her head fell back against the door slightly when his lips and tongue trailed her neck. Alec's hand left her breast, finding the button on her jeans. He was quick to unbutton, unzip and dive under her panties, skimming her oh so teasingly. Marren's lower body pushed towards him, wanting more.

"Nice and warm." Alec continued to fiddle his fingers slowly. His mouth covered Marren's in a seductive, untamed kiss that went on until her breath was stolen. Breaking for air, Alec nibbled her neck, "Should I make you come with my fingers first before I fuck you with my tongue?" Talking to her like that made Marren clench and push into him. He knew the dirty talk excited her and hearing what he planned before he did it made her want it more. His free hand held her waist, feeling the first signs of the heat that would take over her entire body. "You don't need your sweater."

Marren pulled the sweater over her head. No sooner than the sweater was removed and Alec pulled her bra away, his teeth greeted her nipples with bites that were soothed with gentle licks of his tongue. His free hand yanked at the side of her jeans. Alec's fingers slowed, pulling away so he could remove her jeans when Marren clenched his forearm.

She whined, "No, don't stop. Please, I…"

Marren's neck arched when two of Alec's fingers pushed inside. His thumb continued to roll around on the outside while his fingers arched, touching the spot that would undo her. Alec kissed her cheek and over to her ear. He whispered, "My fingers first."

Marren nodded slightly, losing her breath and her mind. He didn't let either return to her before pulling her jeans and panties down and kneeling before her. His mouth and face rubbed across her lower stomach, teasing her until he finished removing her shoes, socks, jeans and panties. Her thigh was pulled up and over his bicep, opening her for the taking. A long, full tongue started at her opening, licking to the place that was always her trigger. He sucked her into his mouth and heard Marren cry out.

"Oh God, please."

He continued until he felt her body jerk and repeated the long, hard pressure of his tongue, tasting her in her entirety. His tongue darted inside over and over, teasing her and turning her on more and more before vacuuming her into his lips where she came undone. Marren whimpered, leading up to a full moan and an "Alec!" at the moment of her release. He kissed up her body then took one step away. His eyes never left hers. Marren's skin was a little damp and her dilated eyes begged for more.

"Lean over the arm of the couch," Alec commanded.

He was not making love at the moment; he was fucking her. She watched him undress himself. Large muscles bounced and when he took his jeans and boxers away, she swallowed hard as she looked at the size of him.

"Go," he commanded, watching her walk to the couch. Marren leaned over the couch and clenched the top with her hand, bracing her body. Alec walked towards her, "Put your knee on the arm."

Marren did as she was told. His hands touched her hips, positioning her to take him.

"You are so fucking beautiful. You make me so hard. Do you know what you do to me?" Alec pressed his hardness against her thigh, letting her feel him. "You're going to let me in deep and hard, aren't you baby?"

His fingers reached around to touch between her legs. Marren's head fell forward from his touch and her bottom pushed towards him, encouraging him to enter her.

"What do you want?" Alec wanted her words.

Marren whimpered, "You."

His fingers continued but he was waiting for her to answer him with a more specific answer. His free hand reached up, taking her hair in his fingers at her scalp.

The soft tug pulled Marren's head back. She exhaled, "Fuck me, Alec."

He pushed in slow but as deep as he could get. Marren moaned, grabbing behind her and holding his hand that was in her hair, "Hard baby. Hard."

Alec pulled out and slammed back inside over and over until he heard moans and soft screams of pleasure from Marren. Her body clamped around him tight, giving him the feel of every pulse. Alec eased the pace a little, working her through the orgasm that left her breathless and fatigued. Feeling the relaxation take her, he pulled out, scooping her up in his arms. Her legs wrapped around his waist and her arms around his neck as her head rested on his shoulder. Walking them to the bedroom, he kissed her forehead.

"You make me feel so good. Two nights are not enough." Marren's face rested in his neck, her nose enjoying the smell of him.

Alec lowered them to the bed and gently eased inside her. His hips rolled slowly, keeping them both euphoric.

He pushed her hair from her face, and looking in her eyes he asked, "How do I feel about you? I want to hear you say it. I want to make sure you know."

Marren's eyes opened, capturing his meaning. "You love me."

His hand held the side of her face while his thumb stroked her cheek, "That's right baby, I love you. I love you so much, Marren. You know that, right?"

Tears filled her eyes with one escaping, falling down the side of her face to her hairline. She nodded. Alec's kiss was complete love, soft, gentle and meaningful. The way he moved his body was the complete opposite of how he worked her over on the couch. Every thrust and stroke he made was thoughtful, every touch loving and in the end, his lovemaking filled her with an exhausting satisfaction. Holding her tight, he whispered, "Hang on to me."

He picked them both up off the bed and walked to the shower. Setting Marren on her feet, he turned the water on to heat. She walked over to the mirror, pulling her hair up and fastening it since she had already washed it that morning.

Alec soaped her body, taking care to caress every inch. "I love this mark." He smiled as he rubbed her lower back, referencing a small birthmark just left of her spine in the shape of what he thought of as lips. "It looks like a permanent kiss."

Marren pressed her face against the tile wall and smiled, "It doesn't look like lips."

Her eyes were closed. She was sleepy, the skating, orgasms and his hands had done her in.

"It does." He kissed her shoulder. "We have time before meeting the guys at the brewery, let's get you dried off and have a quick nap."

Marren nodded.

Stepping out of the shower, Alec pulled a bath sheet, drying Marren and wrapping her up before drying himself with a towel. Hanging both towels, he took Marren by the hand and led them to bed.

Marren sighed heavily, waking to her hair being stroked gently away from her face. Her eyes opened briefly as she looked up at Alec who was watching her sleep on his chest. She lowered her face and closed her eyes.

Alec smiled, "Wake up baby. We have an hour to get to the brewery, unless you want to cancel." His fingers lingered down her back, "I could tell the guys to get their own girl." Alec chuckled, kissing her forehead. "They were upset I didn't invite them out last time you were here, but I'm happy keeping you to myself."

Marren's hand ran up his chest, "We have to eat dinner so we might as well go." Her mouth found his, kissing him with intensity. "You can bring me home early."

"Mmm. You have a deal," Alec smiled.

"Marren!" Six guys yelled from the railing where they could watch the entrance to the bar.

Marren smiled with a wave, "Hey y'all."

Jerry, tall, salt and pepper and handsome walked over, taking her out of Alec's arm by lifting her in a hug off her feet. "My girl's back." Marren giggled. Jerry kept on, "When are you going to dump that ugly jack ass and marry me?"

Marren laughed, "You're not nice."

"I'm honest. Nice and honest don't go hand in hand." Jerry chuckled. He put Marren back on her feet. "Seriously, he's gaining weight, losing his hair, getting older and uglier by the minute." None of which was true, but Jerry had to give Alec shit.

"I'm going to kick your ass," Alec scoffed following them to the bar rail.

All the men hugged Marren, made fun of Alec and teased her with marriage and sex proposals. Marren blushed and laughed while Alec raised his eyebrows with a look of annoyance.

"None of you are true friends," Alec chuckled, pulling Marren back in his arms.

The evening went on with stories of cases, food, drink and fun banter.

"Did he tell you he threw his hat in the ring for lieutenant?" Jerry asked Marren.

Alec cringed, taking a sip of his beer. He knew that he was in trouble for not talking to her about the possible promotion.

Marren smiled a smile that was anything but happy. "He's more than qualified."

Jerry nodded, "That he is. You have to be excited, better pay, and better hours."

Marren took a sip of her beer, "As long as he's happy." She put her beer on the bar. "I'll be right back, the ladies' room is calling."

Marren didn't look at Alec. She picked up her clutch and walked to the bathroom. Alec knew he was headed for an argument.

Marren spent the remainder of the evening talking to the guys, hearing the latest stories of their love lives and listened to them give her a hard time about hand to hand combat and working for the FBI.

"We do all the hard stuff and the FBI swoops in and takes the case." Mike, a new DC detective, complained.

Marren smiled, "Only what is truly ours."

Mike smirked, "Why don't you transfer to DC? It must be boring in Mobile."

"I'm not bored. Plenty of cases. And why come to DC when I get to train newbies in warmer weather?" Marren pressed her lips together. "I have a life beyond the FBI in Fairhope, here it would be all work."

"But you don't get to kick as much ass down south," Mike laughed.

"I kick plenty of ass," Marren laughed.

Mike nodded, "What about this big fucker? Ever get the drop on him?" Mike's thumb gestured to Alec.

"Size doesn't matter. You just need to be a step ahead," Marren winked.

Alec shook his head, "Don't get her started. Your ass will be off your stool faster than you can put your beer down."

Mike laughed, "I'd like to go a couple rounds with you." He bounced his eyebrows at Marren.

Alec smacked Mike in the back of the head, "Watch it."

Marren sat in the passenger seat silently, looking out the window.

Alec glanced at Marren. "My friends love you, more than they love me," Alec said with a smile, hoping to break the silent treatment.

She nodded, "It was nice to see everyone."

"I know what you're thinking. The lieutenant thing, I figure it will open more doors in Fairhope and Mobile for a better position. While I'm here I might as well try to advance, it can only help." When Marren didn't respond, it was clear that she wasn't buying what he was selling. "There hasn't been a good lead on a job in Mobile."

Marren glanced at him, "Christmas, New Year, it looks good. You are not taking time for the holidays since you are up for a promotion.

Everything makes sense. When was the last time you looked for a position in Mobile?"

Alec pulled the car in the garage, "I am looking." Alec sighed, "I couldn't get the time off. What? You don't think I want to be with you for the holidays?"

Marren got out of the car. She walked in the condo, straight to the kitchen for a bottle of water, and then to the bedroom. She was all nighttime business and routine; from brushing her teeth to removing her earrings, she was on task.

Alec watched her while taking off his sweater and jeans. "You going to talk to me?"

"I don't think anything I say matters, so what would be the point?" Marren folded some of her clothes, putting them in her suitcase.

He hated when she packed. "I care what you have to say."

Marren turned looking at him with sad eyes, "Fine. I don't want to live like this. I want to wake up with you in the morning and go to sleep with you at night. Every night. I don't want to spend a weekend together every two to four weeks. We have been doing this for a year and a half. I want more."

"I know what you want. I'm working on it. Look, I'll come to you more after the first of the year. We can work on a better schedule; spend more time together until I find something permanent in Mobile."

Marren looked down, "When do you think you will be in Mobile permanently? What will it take?"

Alec ran his hand over his face and crossed his arms, "I don't know. I'm looking, Ok."

"No Alec, It's not ok. We should be together on Christmas; you should be kissing me at midnight on New Year's Eve, coming home to each other after work. You act like this arrangement is good enough for you. When you delivered the holiday news, it was no big deal to you. I don't believe you are trying very hard to be with me full-time."

Alec was frustrated, "I never said this arrangement is good enough. I miss you as soon as you leave." He shook his head, "What if I was still in the Army? I could be gone for a year at a time. How would you have handled that?" His hand ran through his hair, "You would have been a horrible military wife."

Marren, furious and hurt, started shoving her belongings in her carry on, only leaving her clothes for the following day on the dresser.

"I didn't mean it like that." Alec sighed, "What I'm trying to say is that it could be worse. I am looking and I am trying."

Marren shook her head, "You're not in the army. I want to share my life with someone and you're not going to make me feel guilty about that." Marren walked past him, slamming the bathroom door behind her.

"Fuck." Alec sighed heavy, running his fingers through his hair. He walked to the bathroom door, placing both hands against it. He spoke through the door, calming his voice, "We want the same thing. We are on the same side. It won't be like this forever." Alec waited for Marren to say something. "Come on baby, I don't want our weekend to end like this." Alec paced for a moment then sat on the side of the bed in his boxers, waiting for her.

Marren opened the bathroom door, walking to her side of the bed in a tank top and boy shorts. She plugged in her phone, took a drink of water and got in bed, turning away from Alec. Alec turned the lights off and crawling into bed, he moved behind her. His arm wrapped around her waist, pulling her to him.

"I have been looking. The postings are lateral moves for less money or a step backwards. Something will come up. I want to be with you full-time."

She turned to him, "I could come here. Let's talk about it."

Alec looked at her and shook his head. "I don't want that for you. I know how it was when my sister worked in this field office. You will always be working and have no time for a social life. You have made a name for yourself in Mobile." Alec rolled to his back, bringing her with him to rest on his chest, "We will figure it out."

"You could go private security. Do something else," Marren suggested.

Alec hesitated but said, "I love being a detective. I want to continue in this line of work."

Marren was silent for a long time before she turned away to sleep on her pillow.

Alec stood in the kitchen drinking coffee. He was furious and could feel his heart beat hard in his chest. His phone lit up, letting him know Marren's flight was on time for departure at 1pm. He glanced at the time; it was a little after 8am. Filling his cup again, he heard the sound of the door handle.

"Hey." Marren said, walking in the door, sweaty from her run.

"What the fuck? Why didn't you wake me up if you wanted to run? I would have gone with you," his voice exploded.

She frowned, "You were sleeping. I'm not sure why you're angry, I've gone for a run a thousand times."

Alec shot back, "We go together. This isn't Fairhope. You don't run alone."

Marren rolled her eyes, "Seriously?" She almost laughed at the idea that she needed him to protect her on a run. She had her gun and realistically could take Alec down in a fight, not that she'd ever tried.

"Yes. I'm serious. What are you thinking?" His voice was cocky and barely a step down from his initial explosion.

Marren put her hands on her hips, "I'm thinking you should lower your voice. Talk to me instead of yell at me. I'm capable of handling myself, which you know, so what is the real issue here?"

Alec took a drink of his coffee, "You are leaving in a couple hours and instead of spending that time with me you went for a run by yourself."

Marren shook her head. She was completely flabbergasted. Instead of telling him off, she walked in the bedroom.

Alec followed.

"Are you getting me back for not having the holidays off?" Alec's voice was lower but not less angry.

Marren placed her running shoes in a drawstring bag and put them in her suitcase. "I'm not getting you back for anything. I woke up before you, let you sleep and went for a run. I've done that many times and it has never been a big deal until today."

"Fine. Don't bitch that we don't have much time together if you are going to go it alone when you're here."

Alec was pissed that he woke up and she was gone, plus her voice was settled without any sign of emotion. She was handling him, and he hated that.

Marren looked at him, her voice still calm, "Don't you fucking talk to me like that. I've catered to your schedule for the last year and a half. You are not the only one that has had opportunities and a career." Marren was furious, pausing for a moment, deciding if she would continue.

Keeping her voice level, she went on, "After the first of the year, I'm going to travel some for work. I've been asked to lead training ops and I'm going to do it. I turned it down last fall because I thought..." She looked at Alec, "Who cares what I thought. I need to focus on something other than you. I'm going to re-focus on my career. You should feel relieved, it will take the pressure off you to move to Mobile to be with me. You can keep your ass here and we will meet up when it's convenient for both of us."

"No, you're not! You're only doing that to piss me off." His voice was a boom.

Marren looked at him and with a smart-ass tone she said, "It could be worse, I could be gone for a year. You would be a horrible military husband." She picked up her clothes from the dresser and walked to the bathroom.

When Marren was almost past Alec he shouted, "Where do you think you're going? We are in the middle of an argument."

"What are you arguing with me about? Do you even know? Me going for a run? You waking up without me? Or is it that I'm not pining away for every minute with you this morning?" Marren's glare was brutal. "I've almost begged you to move to Mobile or Fairhope. Pleaded for you to share your life with me. And you're upset because I went for a run without you? What a joke."

Alec watched her walk in the bathroom and shut the door. She might as well have kicked him in the balls.

When it was Alec's turn to shower, he noticed all of her things were put away. He hated Sundays when she had to leave, and this particular one was terrible. Alec knew he was being selfish, wanting everything his way, on his terms, his time frame, but what did she expect? He wasn't going to move in with her without a job. A good job. A job that would provide for her and children. He stepped out of the steamy bathroom wrapped in a towel. Marren was making the bed. She had changed the sheets.

"I didn't ask you to do that." Alec tried to keep the tone of his voice level but failed.

Marren looked up, "I ran the dishwasher. You'll need to put the sheets in the dryer. I didn't want to leave you with everything to do."

Alec was pissed about the sheets, "If I wanted you to change the sheets, I would have asked you to do it."

Marren zipped her carry on and rolled it to the entrance of the condo. Collecting her purse and computer, she used her phone to request an Uber car. She could feel the tears wanting to come but fought hard to keep them back. Marren walked in the kitchen and put the fruit and breakfast food back in the refrigerator. She wanted them to eat together but thought better of it.

"I can't do anything right this morning," she said, feeling Alec's eyes on her. "I called for an Uber. I'm going to the airport early. I'll get something to eat there."

"Don't do that. I'll take you." Alec felt like shit. "The smell of you won't be on the pillowcases. I'm sorry. I wasn't ready to wake up without you next to me."

"I'll text you when I land." She picked up her purse, putting the strap over her shoulder.

"Don't go like this. I'm an asshole. I'm sorry I flipped out this morning." Alec walked to her, placing his hand on the nape of her neck. "I'll take you to the airport. We can talk on the way."

Shaking her head, she said, "I think we both need to cool off before we say anything else. The Uber driver is almost here."

Alec's thumb lifted her chin to look at him. He wished he hadn't. Her eyes were sad and looked at him with a distance that scared him. Alec could tell she was ready to cry.

"Marren, I'm sorry. We will get this figured out."

She didn't say anything, just nodded. His lips pressed against hers.

Alec pulled back from the kiss saying, "I'll get my schedule worked out so I can be in Fairhope for a long weekend right after the New Year."

Marren hugged Alec, pressing her face in the nape of his neck, breathing him in.

"I'll see you." She pulled away, hiding the tears that filled her eyes.

"I love you." He took her back in his arms.

"Love you too."

CHAPTER 3

Marren had done a good job avoiding Alec's calls, satisfying contact with small talk through text messages all week. On Friday, she looked at her phone and read in all caps "CALL ME."

"Hey. I just stepped out for lunch," Marren said after hearing him say hello.

"Me too. I wanted to talk to you about travel dates. I can come in on the Thursday after New Year's Day and leave the following Monday. Think you might be able to take that Friday off? We would have a full three days together."

"That weekend won't work. I'll be in Norfolk for a training op leaving Tuesday. I won't get back until Sunday."

Alec's head was ready to explode. He spoke through gritted teeth. "You knew I was planning to come to you that weekend."

"I don't write the training schedule and I told you I was going to travel for work. We didn't go over dates or make any specific plans so you shouldn't be upset."

"You've never wanted to do that before. You are punishing me for the holidays and not moving to Fairhope. I'm making an effort to spend more time with you." Alec held the phone so tight his knuckles were white.

"Let me drop everything because you've decided to make an effort. This is not all about you, Alec. Contrary to your belief, you're not the only one that has a career that matters. I've passed on opportunities because I've been waiting for you, for us to make a life together." Marren was not going to take any shit from him. She had come home sad, lonely and miserable. She would be spending the holidays without him and she had to do something to fill her life. It was time she figured out what she was going to do for herself besides wait. It was time she became responsible for her own happiness.

"Marren, you are intentionally keeping us from seeing each other. You know traveling with your job right now completely puts us between a rock and a hard place. I don't have every weekend off like you do and if you cut out some of your weekends it limits us even more." Alec paused, "I'm trying to give you what you want, more time."

"I don't want you to give me more time. I want full-time. I deserve more than a negotiation for your time. I deserve a man that would move mountains to kiss me on New Year's Eve. You don't even want me to come there, we could have spent time together before or after your shifts and you made the decision for both of us not to be together. I'm not happy and I don't want this. I want all." Marren felt sick to her stomach.

Alec was speechless for a moment. Stumbling for the right words he said, "I don't want you waiting in the condo on the holidays for me to come home. I figured being with your family or our friends would be better than sitting in the condo alone and waiting. You deserve everything you want, and I know that. I can't give you full-time right now. I'm trying to give you what I can."

Marren swallowed hard. Her throat felt thick. She squeezed her eyes together, hoping to stop them from making tears. The silence on the phone felt like minutes but in reality, it was only seconds. The silence was the hope that was fading, the hope that one of them would back down, but neither could.

Alec spoke gently, "I love you but if I don't make you happy… What should I do, let you go? Is that what you want? I don't want you to be unhappy. I don't want to be without you but giving you all is not possible for me right now."

"Ok." Marren heard her voice sound small and upset.

"You want me to let you go?" Alec couldn't believe what was happening. He thought saying that would stop her in her tracks.

Marren fought to sound like she wasn't crying but her voice sounded like she would have a complete melt down at any moment, "It's not fair for you to feel pressured to do something you can't and it's not fair for me to wait for you to do something I don't think you will ever do. I don't believe we want the same thing. I think you are content with the way things are and I'm not."

Alec couldn't believe his ears, "Baby, I will move to Fairhope for you. I need a job to do that. We want the same thing."

Marren's tears were flowing steady, "If we wanted the same thing, you wouldn't have applied for a promotion in DC."

"I told you why I did that. Look, I know what I've been doing doesn't look like I'm trying to be with you. Let's just get through the holidays and…"

Marren interrupted, "No. I can't hope anymore. I can't." Her voice sounded on the verge of sobbing.

Alec felt desperate, "Baby, don't cry. I'll fix this."

"No you won't. You could have already if you were going to. We don't love each other the same. We need to let it go."

Marren was sobbing and at this point she didn't care.

"Marren." Alec felt his heart sink.

"I need to let it go. I love you but I can't do this anymore." Marren tried to calm her voice.

Alec sighed. His thumb and index fingers rubbed his eyebrows as he squinted. "Don't do this. Let me come there and let's talk in person. I don't want to be without you."

"You are without me most of the time and managing just fine." Marren wiped her tears.

Both silent and shocked, they held the phones for several long moments, waiting for the other to say something, anything to confirm that this was not really happening.

"I've got to go." Marren hung up the phone.

She spent her lunch hour crying then trying to clean up her face, only to cry again. She finally got it together, returning to work late.

Marren was unusually quiet at yoga. She heard Jubileigh, Paisley, Ophelia and Addison talking and laughing but wasn't really listening to the conversations. It was Wednesday and she hadn't left her house since coming home the previous Friday from work. Marren couldn't remember ever feeling this distraught or lost. She took three personal days and was due back to work the next morning. Getting out tonight seemed like a good idea, giving herself a test run on not having a complete melt down in public.

"So, are you and Alec going to meet us in Florida for Christmas or are you going to stay at your place?" Addison asked Marren.

Marren was a million miles away.

"Earth to Marren," Addison giggled. "You must be feeling the inner peace."

Marren smiled, "I'm sorry. What did you say?

Addison repeated the question.

"I'm going to Minneapolis for the holidays." Marren switched positions when the instructor gave the direction.

Addison could tell something was not right, "You and Alec could come for New Year's Eve. Split the holidays up so you are in warmer weather."

"Alec is going to be in DC. He's working the holidays."

Addison noticed Marren avoiding eye contact. "I bet you're pissed about that. I would be. Can you guys do the holidays in DC with Alec's buddies?"

Marren shook her head, "He didn't offer that." Marren released her pose and stood. "Alec and I are not together anymore. I'm not feeling very zen. I'm going to take off." Marren bent over, rolling up her mat.

All of the women stopped.

"We can all go. Let's get a beer and talk."

"I don't want to talk about it. It's for the best. Really, I just need some sleep. I'm exhausted. I'll see everyone over the weekend." Marren didn't give anyone a chance to argue with her, she took her mat and headed for the door.

Addison hurried, walking behind her, "Marren, wait. I'll come over. We can talk about it. I'm here for you."

Marren shook her head, "I can't talk about it." Marren's eyes filled with tears. "He's your brother and it's not fair for you to be in the middle. I don't want that. I'll be ok. I'm going to work and stay busy. I'll call you this weekend." Marren stepped up, giving Addison a quick hug before getting in her car.

"Hey Addie."

"What the fuck did you do?" Addison barked at her brother.

Alec blew out a deep breath, his voice low and sad. "So you heard? Was I a topic at yoga?"

"Marren's been blowing me off since she got back from DC last week. Tonight was the first time I've seen her or talked to her. She said you are working the holidays when I asked about you guys coming to Florida. When I pushed for New Year's, she told me you've broken up. That's all she will say. I wish you were a topic tonight, at least then she would talk to me. So you tell me, what happened?"

Alec told Addison about the weekend and then the break up conversation on Friday. "Look Addie, I don't want it this way. I can't believe it's over. I spent the majority of my weekend drunk. I'm miserable without her. I left a voicemail for her Monday evening begging her to reconsider, asking her to give me a little more time to get something worked out. She hasn't replied. I called her at work, her cell, texted; she won't talk to me."

"Get your ass on a plane," Addison directed.

"I can't. We are short staffed because of vacations. I'm working overtime for the next three weeks."

Addison shook her head, "You realize this is the reason you lost her? Putting work before her, not getting your ass here; what are you doing? Do you think you are ever going to meet someone like Marren again? You're willing to lose her? Damn Alec, she's been waiting for you to make a move for a long time."

"I know. You think I don't know that? I love her. I want her for my life, but I have to have a job lined up and not a shit job." Alec paused, "How was she?"

"Quiet. She looks upset and sad. How do you think she is?" Addison was annoyed.

Alec closed his eyes, "I don't want her upset. I want to work this out. She has to talk to me in order to do that. I'll keep trying her by phone. As soon as I can come there, I plan to. I want to be in Fairhope with her. I'll get it figured out."

"You keep saying that. You need to do more doing and less saying."

Alec sighed, "I hear you."

CHAPTER 4

M arren Quinn walked through the County Building in Mobile Alabama like she had many times since taking the promotion and transfer five years prior to the FBI's local field office. Checking on a state criminal case that was expected to make its way to federal court was a perfect reason to be indoors, out of the August heat and humidity.

She blended in, looking like many of the people roaming the halls in a dark navy suit, white shirt, not too high heels and a badge, letting everyone know who she was. Keeping with the professional look, her hair was parted on the right side and pulled back in a pretty knot at the back of her head. Out of work her thick, dark brown, hair would fall in layers to the middle of her back, giving her back the feminine look that she preferred. Marren was blessed with a beautiful complexion, pouty pink lips, and long eyelashes so it was easy to keep her make-up modest for work. She wore tailored suits but never purchased anything that would get her noticed as sexy or make men see her as beautiful because she had to be taken seriously.

Being a young female FBI agent, her skills and professional manner meant everything. Playing down natural beauty was impossible, which intimidated some men. She was gorgeous without trying, smart, and accomplished at thirty-five. Even more intimidating, she was deadly.

She had a solid reputation and in the last eight months she had traveled consistently, conducting training ops nationally and earning the recognition that she deserved. Marren's occupation was a gun range and hand-to-hand combat instructor for the FBI. She knew her job and knew it well.

Walking through the county building she received nods from local police officers, lawyers and co-workers alike. Marren felt satisfied with her career, eight years with the bureau was nothing to sneeze at.

Speaking to another agent, Marren watched a familiar figure step in one of the hearing rooms.

"I'll catch up with you," she smiled, turning to follow Alec Jacobs into the room.

The room was set up with multiple pews for seating, all of which were taken. It was standing room only, so she moved to the side, watching Alec maneuver his way towards the front and drop off paperwork. She looked at her watch, noticing it was 10am, which meant Alec must have flown in to Mobile at least the day before. It was Wednesday and she wondered why he wasn't at work.

Alec was living in DC still. She only knew that because Addison would drop subtle hints about her brother, hoping to keep things alive. Marren heard he took the lieutenant position, the one he applied for before they broke up. Since they had mutual friends, she did see him from time to time at functions that he was in town for, but she had managed to keep her distance, refusing to talk to him.

"Brew and Burger Fairhope," an announcement was made from the liquor license commissioner.

Alec stood up, making his way to the lectern. Marren listened to Alec describe the new business and location. The opening was planned first quarter of the following year, giving six to seven months for build out and inspections. After only fifteen minutes of particulars being discussed, the liquor license was approved.

Marren's head was spinning. She assumed Max, a chef and Addison's husband, was involved, and maybe even the rest of the guys from their group. Seth, Ophelia's husband owned a popular and successful bar and Brogan, Max's partner, franchised a restaurant chain of twenty-six locations; they would all be good business partners with Alec. Marren could feel the heat come to her face, feeling angry and hurt. Being angry or feeling anything about Alec made her even more upset. She didn't want to care one way or the other what the man was up to.

She watched Alec walk out the door, following after him.

A few steps behind, Marren called, "Alec."

Alec heard Marren's voice say his name and he closed his eyes briefly. Alec knew there was a possibility she would be in the building for her job but was hoping he would miss her.

He turned, "Hi Marren. How are you?"

Damn she was beautiful. She looked all business and beautiful.

Marren's face looked concerned, "A liquor license?"

Alec continued to walk, keeping pace with Marren next to him. He did not look at her when he said, "Business investment."

"Why? Why Fairhope and why now?" Marren's voice showed signs of agitation.

Alec glanced at her, "Why haven't you returned any of my phone calls in eight months? Why is it that every time I try to talk to you, you refuse?" Alec stopped and looked at her. She stopped but only met his eyes for a moment before looking away. "Come on Marren. I've tried to see you so many times. I've called, texted, sent flowers, left notes. You snubbed me at Ophelia's mom's funeral, sitting directly across from me for drinks after the wake and didn't say a word to me, then the

Fourth of July party, complete silence. Let me take you to lunch and I'll tell you about the brewery. We can talk about what happened between us."

Marren stiffened, "Good luck with your business investment." Marren turned, walking in a different direction and getting lost in a sea of police officers.

Alec walked in Bone and Barrel at 6pm on Wednesday night. The guys, Max, Seth, and Brogan were meeting Alec to celebrate the approval of the liquor license for their new venture, and the girls would be joining them after yoga. They each had a drink and talked business and next steps for an hour before Max announced he and Addison were expecting their first child. The guys congratulated Max and set up a celebration for the next night so everyone would be in attendance. Miller and Paisley, close friends of the group, had brought their new baby girl, Grayce, home from the hospital just a few weeks earlier. They hadn't been doing much with the group but would want to be included in the celebration.

When the girls arrived, Marren was not with them.

Addison sat down. "I'm assuming she figured you would be here since you ran into each other at the county building. She asked what you are up to."

"What did you tell her? I told her she needed to talk to you." Addison was not happy.

She and Marren were close friends and the break-up had put a strain on the friendship.

"I tried to talk to her today and she wouldn't. I don't know what else to do." Alec was at a complete loss.

Addison looked at him, "It's not like her to be unreasonable. I can't get her to talk about you or your relationship. I don't get it."

Alec took a drink of his beer, "I'll see her tomorrow night. We are going out to celebrate your bun in the oven."

CHAPTER 5

M arren looked at her reflection in the mirror before she left to go to the celebration dinner and drinks for Addison and Max. She could only hope that Alec had to go back to DC for work but figured that would be too good to be true. If she had to see him, she was going to look gorgeous, happy and like she didn't have a care in the world. She wore a bright blue shirt that fell off one shoulder; the fit showed off her breasts. Her shorts were black and sexy, hitting high on the thigh and her long legs looked even better with her high heeled black sandals. Marren checked out her butt in the mirror, it was nice in the shorts. She stood 5'8 without heels. Size 8. Her body was soft in the right areas but from her work at the FBI she was strong and muscular where she needed to be. She smiled, knowing she would turn heads in the outfit. Her hair was down, silky with bouncing layers; it looked touchable. She reapplied her lipstick and walked out the door, getting in her car. Her new home was within walking distance of the Fly Bar where everyone was meeting but the August humidity in Fairhope Alabama was horrible, so she drove her car to stay cool with air conditioning.

When she arrived she was happy to see an open seat at the opposite end of the table from Alec. She sat next to Paisley and asked her all about new mom life. Marren tried to get lost in conversation to avoid Alec and his intense stare. She made eye contact with him once briefly when Brogan talked about the new brewery venture. Brogan mentioned that Alec was leading the charge dealing with the contractor and inspections that were coming up in the next few months.

When Alec was asked about moving to Fairhope he nodded, "Looks like I will officially be in Fairhope full-time by the end of the year. The brewery has been in the works since January so I've been preparing for it to be my only full-time job but I accepted a position as SWAT team lead for the Field Operations Division in Mobile, replacing the current team lead when he retires in January. Looks like I'll join the majority of everyone here with two careers," Alec smiled.

"Congratulations. Great timing, you are going to have a ton to celebrate next year. New job, brewery and being an uncle!" Max reached over, giving him a pat on the shoulder.

Everyone congratulated Alec with Marren simply forcing a smile and a nod. She was thrilled when Jubileigh talked about the new gallery that she had just opened and how much fun she was having being back in Fairhope. Unfortunately, Jubileigh's ex-husband decided to crash the party. Chris Wiseman interrupted the group causing a small scene but nothing that was overheard by anyone besides the table of friends. Jubileigh stood to deal with Chris with Brogan and Miller, Jubileigh's brother, keeping a watchful eye on the situation.

It was then that Alec looked at Marren, "We need to talk."

Most everyone was paying attention to Jubileigh and Chris having words, but Alec was ready to have words with her.

Marren rolled her eyes, *No we don't.* She mouthed without noise. She could see Alec simmering over her response.

Marren sat for the next hour pretending to listen to the conversations around her, all the while thinking back to the last weekend she spent with Alec. How he changed the subject every time she brought up moving to Fairhope or what direction their relationship was going. She remembered how hurt she was getting on the plane, the tears she shed when she got in her bed alone that night. The hardest decision she made was calling it quits. Marren remembered his words when they broke up, "If I don't make you happy, should I let you go." He let her go. She meant so little to him, he let her go. Thank God the night was wrapping up.

She hugged Addison and Max, "I'm so happy for both of you. I'm available for babysitting; just throwing that out there early." Marren had a genuine smile on her face.

"Are you leaving? Come to Bone and Barrel. It's early," Addison pouted.

"I have an early morning," Marren answered.

She always had an early morning so that was not the issue. There was no way she was going to spend a second more in the presence of Alec.

"I'm parked that way, I'll walk with you." Marren waited for Addison to say good-bye and the girls walked towards Bone and Barrel with Max and Alec following. When they reached the door of the bar Marren smiled, hugging Addison again, "See you this weekend."

"I'll walk you to your car," Alec stated. It wasn't really an offer. He was walking her to her car.

"I've got it. I'm right there." Marren pointed to her car parked six parking spaces to the right of the entrance.

"I'll walk you," Alec insisted.

Marren smiled through gritted teeth, "Go enjoy yourself, you have reason to celebrate. I'm fine. I don't want you to walk me to my car."

Alec took Marren by the arm. His grip wasn't tight, just leading. Marren pulled her arm away but continued to walk. Addison watched, knowing there was going to be an explosion.

"What is your problem?" Alec's voice was angry. "I want to explain the move and job."

Marren met him with just as much anger in her voice, "I don't want you to explain. I don't have a problem. We don't need to do this."

Alec smirked, "We obviously need to do something. Look, you broke up with me. You're acting like I am the bad guy. I wanted to work things out and you didn't. You're pissed. You've been pissed for months so let's have it out."

Marren shook her head, "You really want to do this?" She waited a moment for Alec to say something, what she received was a cocky, angry look on his face and a raised eyebrow, so she proceeded. "You're the one pissed off? Pissed I'm not jumping for joy that a fucking beer and cheeseburger got you to move here? I'm so happy for you, enjoy brewing beer and flipping hamburgers. Get the hell out of my way." Marren tried to step around him but he blocked the driver's door of her car.

Alec nodded, trying to hold back the laugh from the *flipping burgers* comment. He had to hand it to her; she delivered one-liners like a professional smart ass.

"I needed an income to move here; that's where the brewery idea came from. Max and I got the idea when he visited DC. Look, I've wanted to talk to you about this for a long time."

"I haven't wanted to hear anything from you for a long time. Please get out of my way." Marren again stepped to get in her car but he wouldn't let her.

"Why? I understand why you broke it off. I got the message. You wanted us to be together full-time. I've been trying to make that happen."

"You are not doing this for me. Christ, I waited for you to make an effort, any effort, half-ass look for a job here, and you did nothing. You sidestepped every conversation. Almost two years of dating and you couldn't pull the trigger, so don't do it now." Marren was furious.

"I did look for a job here. The entire time we dated. Anything that came up was a step down. Having a conversation about a job that wasn't available would only make things that much worse. I know you, you wouldn't have cared if it was a step down, but I did. I wasn't going to take a job and not be able to provide for you."

Marren went from furious to upset quickly, "So it was better to break my heart?" She hesitated, "I was in love with you Alec. I wanted to spend my life with you. You wouldn't even talk to me. Do you remember our last weekend together? I left in tears because the next time we could see each other was almost a month away. You acted like it wasn't a big deal. You went so far as to make fun that I wouldn't have been a good military wife because you were gone for long lengths of time when you were enlisted."

Alec ran his hand over his face, "that was a dick thing for me to say. I'm sorry I did that. I was trying to make it seem like we weren't going to be apart that long."

Marren shook her head, "It wasn't that big of a deal for you. It wasn't that long for you. You didn't care that you would go weeks without seeing me."

"Of course I cared. You think I wanted it that way? I wanted you with me. Do you think being away from you has been easy on me? I miss you. I ache to touch you. I am here for you. I want another chance with you."

Hearing those words and not believing them, tears fell from Marren's eyes, "After we broke up," Marren wiped the tears from her cheeks, "I called you three days later. I was so heartbroken. I couldn't take it anymore. I just wanted you and decided to hell with my house and Fairhope, I was coming to DC. I was on my way to work Monday morning and planned to ask for the transfer. I was in the car, it was 6am, and I wanted to tell you my plans. I knew you would be up and getting ready for work." Marren sniffed, "But you didn't answer your cell phone, a woman answered, she said you were in the shower."

Alec swallowed hard.

"You fucked someone the same weekend we broke up, that's how much you missed me. That's how much I meant to you." Marren choked out the words through her tears. "I would have given up my life here and you had already found a warm body."

"It wasn't like that," Alec said quietly in a panic. "Marren, it wasn't like that."

Marren looked at him, "You didn't have another woman in your bed three days after we broke up?"

"I went out and got drunk for three days. I was a mess thinking I lost you. I don't even remember leaving the bar that night. I fucked up. I'm so sorry." Alec reached for her hand.

Marren pulled away, "If you don't move out of my way, I'm going to move you out of my way. I don't care where you live or what you do. Just stay away from me."

"I love you, Marren. Two weeks in and I was head over heels in love with you. I still am. I screwed up. I'm sorry. I know I hurt you, I will never..."

Marren shoved him away from her car door, "Don't say another word to me." She got in her car and drove away, hysterical.

Alec's hand raked his face. He stood with his eyes closed next to the empty parking space for a long moment. When he turned, his sister stood ten feet away with her hands on her hips. Max walked in the bar, not wanting to hear what Addison was going to say to him.

Alec looked like he had been run over by a car, "Did you know she called me?"

Addison shook her head, "No. She's been carrying that around for months. Never said a word. You are a fucking idiot. How could you do that? I've never seen her upset like this. I'm going to her house. You and Max will need to call an Uber or walk home." Addison dug in her purse for car keys.

A huge sigh left Alec, "I was so wasted. I don't even remember taking the girl home. The next morning, I wake up and she's in my bed. I got in the shower for work." Alec paused. "I was hurting over Marren and went on a three-day bender. I know it's shitty. I will do anything to make this right."

"How do you make fucking someone else right?" Addison shook her head. "You have really screwed up. I don't know if she will ever forgive you. Broken up or not, do you realize what that looks like? Exactly like what she said, like you replaced her three days later; like she didn't mean shit to you. Damn Alec, I don't think you deserve her."

Alec looked at her, "Trust me you don't need to beat me up over it. I know what it looks like. I don't deserve her. Addie, I love her. I don't think I will ever get over her. I have to try to win her back."

Addison stalked off to her car.

Alec walked in Bone and Barrel. Max had a beer waiting for him.

"Shot?" Max offered.

Alec gave a nod.

Max signaled the bartender, "Two shots of Jack."

There was nothing to clink glasses for. Both men slung the whiskey back.

"You have royally fucked up," Max said, putting his glass down. "All the women will band together. If we defend you, we are fucked. If

I say that you fucked up, my wife will jump to your defense. I'm screwed either direction." Max signaled the bartender, "Two more."

"Addie pretty much told me I'm a piece of shit that doesn't deserve Marren. I agree with her. She called me an idiot and she looked at me like our mom did when she was disappointed in our behavior."

"I know that look. It's awful. It makes you feel like you are something to be scraped off a shoe." Max felt the buzz coming on from the shot.

"Thanks buddy. I knew I could count on you to make me feel better," Alec commented.

Max shook his head tipping back the second shot of Jack; "There is no making you feel better. I'm just keeping it real by getting you drunk. Want me to lie?"

Alec shook his head, "You know Marren and I agreed to date other people at one point in our relationship because of the long distance, but I never did." Alec took the second shot of Jack. "I only wanted to be with her. Nobody has ever compared to Marren." Alec signaled the bartender for two more shots.

"Who was the girl?" Max asked.

"Someone I took out on a couple dates like five years ago. I don't remember talking to her at the bar. I was so fucking embarrassed the next morning. I apologized, explained the drinking. She said she was getting over a breakup and had too much to drink as well." Alec shook his head, "I hate that I hurt Marren over a drunken mistake. Fuck, I didn't think anyone would know about it. I'm so fucking humiliated."

The third shot went down. It wasn't long before both men were feeling no pain.

Addie pulled up in Marren's driveway and got out of the car. She knocked on the door, "It's Addie. I'm alone."

Marren opened the door in a tank top and pajama bottoms. Her hair was pulled back in a ponytail. Eyes red.

Addie hugged Marren, "Why didn't you tell me? You've been hurting over this for so long. I don't care that Alec is my brother. I'm your best friend. You should have told me. He is a fucking idiot for doing what he did. He was wrong, about not moving here, about letting you go, about the drinking bender, about the girl. You are the best thing that has ever happened to Alec and he screwed it up."

Marren sobbed, "I just want to be over him. Over what he did." Marren cried in Addison's shoulder.

Addison walked them in the kitchen, "What do you have to drink?"

"You can't drink," Marren objected.

"Not for me silly. I'm going to fix you a drink and we are going to sit down and talk this through. Figure out how to get you on the other side of it."

CHAPTER 6

The next morning Addison started banging pans around as loud as she could in the kitchen, getting ready to prepare omelets for breakfast. She knew Max and Alec would be hung over. Max smelled like a distillery when he came to bed hiccupping.

Her husband walked out of their bedroom in a t-shirt and shorts. He didn't say a word, just headed for the coffee.

Alec on the other hand came out of the guest room annoyed. "Really? Max is never that loud making breakfast."

Addison smiled, "I'm not making you breakfast. Did you get drunk last night? Do you have an over-night guest I should know about?"

Max almost spit out his coffee, "Alec, coffee?"

Alec looked at Max, "Sure." Then he looked at his sister, "Addison, that was low."

"She should have decked you. The more I think about you hurting her the more I want to deck you." Addison looked at both of the men. They looked like shit. She threw the pan in the sink. The rattle was so loud both men cringed. "Make your own damn breakfast both of you! Drunk fools!" Addison stormed out of the kitchen to the bedroom.

Max looked at Alec, "I told you. I didn't do anything and she's pissed at me." Max shook his head. He opened the refrigerator and pulled out V-8. "This will help with the hangover." He reached in the cabinet for Advil, "This too." Both men took Advil, drank a glass of V-8, a glass of water, and went back to bed.

Max lay down on the bed while Addison changed her clothes. "Why are you angry with me exactly?" His hand pressed on his temples, trying to pressure the pain away.

"Men are so stupid," Addison said, putting in her earrings.

Max gave a half smirk, "I'm not saying I don't agree with you. I'm just wondering why I'm in trouble. I haven't said anything about the situation yet."

"Let me guess, you are going to defend him?" Addison stood with her hands on her hips looking at Max who was on his back with his arm now shielding the daylight from his eyes.

"Uh, I haven't said anything, so maybe kiss me or rub my head. I feel like crap. Remember you love me?" Max half smiled.

Addison smiled, "I love you. You did too many shots, that's the only time you wake with a hangover."

"Correct. I need you to talk softer. Come love on me." Max tried to persuade Addison.

Addison walked over to the side of the bed and kissed his forehead. "You taste and smell like whiskey. A hot shower will help. What is my brother going to do about Marren?"

"We have no plan of action." Max was miserable.

Addison huffed, "Why not?"

"Because we drank and talked about how bad he fucked up. We couldn't get past that to come up with a plan to fix it. As shitty as it was, they were broken up. He'll come up with something."

"That is such a guy thing to say." Addison sounded disgusted.

Max opened one eye, "I'm a guy; a very hung over guy. Maybe we should talk about this when my head is not pounding."

"Fine!" Her voice was loud.

She grabbed her shoes and stormed out of the bedroom.

"Addison, get back in here." Max sat on the edge of the bed waiting for her.

Addison walked back in the bedroom.

"You and I are not going to get into an argument over something your brother did. I know it's a guy mentality versus a girl mentality about them being broken up. I feel bad for both of them. He is miserable over Marren. He has been miserable for months, without even knowing she knew about the drunken mistake. I know she's hurt. You and I, we feel bad for both of them. We love them both. We want them both to be happy. Your brother is a good man that made a mistake." Max nodded. "Does that separate me from the typical guy thing to say?"

Addison nodded, "Yes." She walked, over wrapping him in a hug.

Max leaned against her, "I feel like shit. I have to work tonight at The Pillars."

She kissed his forehead, "Take a hot shower and go back to sleep. I'll bring you another bottle of water; that should fix it for work. I'm going to take Marren out for lunch. I love you."

"I love you too." Max got up, walking to the bathroom as Addison walked out of the bedroom. Alec was sitting on a barstool in the kitchen when Addison entered.

"Don't be pissed at him because you're pissed at me."

"I'm not." Addison slipped her sandals on. She took two water bottles out of the refrigerator, handing one to Alec.

Alec nodded, "How was she last night?"

"Awful. I think she has convinced herself that you didn't think much of your relationship and that you didn't really love her." Addison walked in the bedroom, placing the water bottle on the nightstand for Max to drink when he got out of the shower.

She returned to the kitchen, "I'm going to see if Marren will go to lunch. She took a personal day."

"I fly to DC tonight. I need to see her before I go," Alec said.

Addison looked at him, "Not sure how you're going to do that. Call her and hope she answers?"

"You know she won't answer. Give me her new address," Alec asked.

Addison shook her head, "No, I'm not going to do that to her. If she wanted you to have her address, she would have given it to you. You're on your own."

Alec decided his best chance was to leave Marren a voicemail: "Marren, please answer the phone and talk to me. Please let me see you. I'm sorry. I'm so sorry I hurt you. Please forgive me. I made a mistake, a terrible mistake." He paused. "I was in love with you every minute. I wanted to share my life with you then and I want to share my life with you now. I was devastated that we broke up. I loved you when we were together. I love you now. Please don't doubt that. You meant the world to me, still do. I wish I could go back and do it different. I was a fool to ever let you go. Please talk to me." Alec could hear the pleading in his voice, knowing that she would be the only reason he would plead or beg for anything.

His call went unanswered.

CHAPTER 7

S eth gave Alec a nod when he took a seat at the bar rail. Bone and Barrel was the place to be. It was 5pm on the Thursday before Halloween and the annual Witches Ride was going to get started at 5:30pm. The witches were pre-drinking for the ride.

Alec smiled at Seth, "Interesting."

Seth laughed, "That it is. I love it. Every year women get dressed up as witches and ride their bikes around, stopping for drinks all evening. It's cool. Did you see the girls? My sister, Shelby, is with them." Seth signaled with his head to the women sitting at a table across the walking aisle from the bar rail. They were all there except Addison, who was sitting out this year because of her pregnancy.

Alec turned on his stool, taking a drink of his beer. He laughed. The women looked hot, witchy hot, but just the same. Alec turned back to talk to Seth.

"Go over and say hi. You haven't seen my sister since the 4th of July." Seth acknowledged.

"Don't you think that's walking into the lion's den? I'm sure none of them are happy to see me, especially Marren. I want her to have a good time and not spoil it for her." Alec took a drink of his beer. "The electrical was approved. Did I mention that? The inspection went well today."

Seth nodded, "That's good news. The inspector came in for a burger a while ago, so I heard from him." Seth laughed, "Small town. You'll get used to it. I don't think the women will turn you into a toad if you go over."

Alec smirked, "Right small town. I don't think you're right about the toad thing."

"Hey, Addison told me to be on the lookout for you." Ophelia approached the bar, giving Alec a hug. "You enjoying the people watching?" She laughed, "It gets better, wait until we all get a few drinks in us and try to ride those bikes."

"You look great. Addie told me a little about this, but it is more than I thought it would be." Alec smiled. "Down side of being pregnant, she couldn't drink her way through town on a bike, so they decided to visit Max's parents this week."

"Next year, Marren has Jubileigh riding the tandem bike with her. You coming over to say hi?" Ophelia asked.

"Not a good idea. I'm sure Marren would prefer I stay where I am. She deserves to have fun. I don't want to ruin that." Alec took another sip of his beer.

"Still hasn't answered your calls?" Ophelia raised an eyebrow.

Alec shook his head, "I did get a couple text message replies. 'Stop texting me', and two of my personal favorites, 'Go flip a cheeseburger' and 'We were on a break has already been used by a sitcom so screw you'. Alec gave a concerned smile, "Last night after yoga, I was hoping when you all were here she would talk to me but she didn't."

Ophelia couldn't hold back a small laugh, "I know this situation is not funny, lots of hurt, but she is entertainin'. We don't get to hear any of this. Marren will not talk about you one way or the other. Anything I know is from Seth and a few things Addie has commented on. Maybe get her talking after she's had a drink or two tonight?"

Alec laughed, "I'm sure she'll tell me what she really thinks with a couple drinks in her. I think I'll pass. I'll figure something out. You girls have fun."

It was nearing 9:30pm when Seth looked at his phone, "Let's head over to Fly Bar. Ophelia said the girls are at their last stop."

Brogan, Alec, Miller and Seth walked over to Fly Bar, just a block from Bone and Barrel. The small bar was packed and the girls were laughing, whooping it up with large, fish bowl looking drinks in front of them.

Miller leaned to Alec, "Oh Lord that drink does them all in." He laughed, walking to his wife, Paisley and giving her a kiss.

Ophelia walked over with two men following her. "Tim and Jared stopped in for a drink," she said. Ophelia looked at Alec, "You know Tim?"

Alec shook Tim's hand, "Nice to see you." He knew that Tim worked with Marren at the FBI, same expertise. They partnered frequently.

Tim responded with the same. "This is Jared Mullins. He works organized crime."

"Good to meet you," Alec nodded.

Tim smiled, "I guess this is the night to be in Fairhope." He looked around the bar at the forty-plus women dressed like sexy witches.

Everyone laughed.

"Yes, it is," Ophelia agreed. "Join us girls." Ophelia lead the way to the corner that the women had claimed so she could get back to her drink.

"What is with the size of that drink?" Alec laughed, asking Seth.

Seth raised an eyebrow, "It's become a tradition that they drink the 'Dragon's Eye' at the end of the ride. It's a combination of liquor and sweet sparkling wine. The girls love it and when I get Ophelia home, I become a fan as well," Seth chuckled.

"Gotcha." Alec made eye contact with Marren. She seemed less ready to pull out her gun and shoot him than earlier when he looked at her. He stepped closer, "How was the ride?"

"Fun." She took a sip of her drink.

Alec's lips pressed together with a nod. "You look great. Very festive."

Marren sat up a little straighter, "Every year it's a new look. Last year's outfit was purple and black. I went with green and black this year."

"How did the hat stay on when you were riding?" Alec asked, seeing that all the women had removed their hats, piling them up on the counter top.

"Bobby pins. After the first bar, they get in the way so they come off for the rest of the night." Marren touched her hair, making sure it was in place.

"You're perfect." Alec smiled, referencing her quick check of her appearance.

Marren's eyes met his for a lingering look of what he could only describe as a mixture of want and hostility.

"I don't fly home until Sunday. Can I see you? Talk over some coffee or a meal? Completely platonic, I heard you're seeing someone."

His sister told Alec that Jared Mullins, who he just met, took Marren out on a couple dates last month. He figured he would throw it out there to see her reaction.

Marren frowned, "Addison has a big mouth."

Alec laughed, "That's a given. Sad part, she's proud of it."

"I'm dating. I'm sure you are too. As for this weekend, I have a ton of work at the house that I'm trying to get accomplished."

Alec sighed at yet another rejection, "I'm not dating anyone. I could help with the house. We could talk while we work."

Marren shook her head, "There's nothing to talk about. It is what it is. Obviously we can be friendly towards one another, this conversation didn't end in tears or weapons being drawn. Let's just leave it be."

Alec's lips curved into an almost smile. He gave her a thoughtful look.

His fingers touched her arm as he leant his body in so he could talk in her ear, "I know you still feel the same chemistry I do. I see the way you look at me. There is something to talk about. I won't leave it be. I'm never going to just walk away."

Marren stood up from the bar stool, forcing Alec to step back. "You are full of yourself. I don't feel anything." Her voice was loud enough for only him to hear. "I was trying to be nice and you have to go all cocky. Take your smug attitude and find a girl that will find that attractive. You arrogant ass."

Alec nodded, leaning in again, knowing he was making her uncomfortable with how close he stood. "If you don't feel what I do, what is the problem with sitting down with me and letting me say my peace? You're scared to be alone with me. I love you and I want you. There is nothing that I wouldn't do to get you back. Tell me what to do."

"I'm not scared. I just don't want to."

Marren stepped away towards the other women, making it impossible for any additional conversation. Alec backed off, joining Seth, Brogan and Miller.

"She's tough. How did it go?" Brogan asked.

"I'm talking to you right now instead of her." Alec took a long pull of his beer.

Brogan gave him a pat on his back, "She talked to you. More than what she's been doing."

The conversation moved to business and included Tim and Jared. Jared talked about being in Chicago for the last six weeks under cover. He was only back for two days to handle briefings and a meeting with the Special Agent in charge on the direction of the investigation.

"I'm ready to be back in Mobile. Don't get me wrong, I like the case and the work is interesting but damn it's cold. The wind cuts right through you. Chicago is already showing signs of winter."

The guys laughed.

Alec added, "I'm looking forward to not having a DC winter. I don't envy you in Chicago. When do you think you will wrap up?"

"At the rate this is going and what is being discovered, no time soon. I ordered a winter coat," Jared smirked.

Alec liked the guy. He sized him up a little, noticing he was almost as tall and fit. Alec had a little size on him, but Jared didn't look like someone to be messed with.

"I had this meeting and when the opportunity to see Marren came up I dragged Tim over here tonight."

Not only did Tim work with Marren but he was also very good friends with her. He knew a little of the situation with Alec.

He was quick to change the subject, "Yeah I was really dragged over here, kicking and screaming," Tim chuckled, "these women are hot. I never knew witches could look so naughty."

Everyone laughed.

"When will you be in Fairhope full-time? Tim was telling me about the brewery," Jared asked Alec.

"I closed on my house yesterday so officially with a home in thirty days. The brewery is on track and we will have a grand opening in late February. I start with the Mobile PD in January. I'm cashing in my vacation time with the DC PD so I'll be here the month of December moving in and getting situated." Alec took a drink of his beer.

Jared nodded, "I hear the FBI is planning a joint task force early next year with the Mobile PD for training and support to get some of the bad areas cleaned up."

Alec nodded, "March first SWAT will be working with the FBI. It should be interesting. I don't know any details yet."

"Marren is leading the training, combat and fire arms. Mobile has some issues with some over zealous officers. The police chief wants things cleaned up. The pressure is coming from the mayor. The program is being designed to train on not brutalizing or shooting to kill. You're right, it should be interesting," Jared explained.

Alec didn't say anything, just listened.

"You are walking into a hornet's nest. Few bad seeds that IA hasn't been able to make yet," Tim added.

"I'm aware of that. Part of my directive when I took the position was to flush out the shit. I'm looking forward to kicking the nest." Alec turned, placing his beer on the bar.

When he turned back around, Jared had walked over to the group of women. He watched Jared talking Marren up for a few moments.

Alec nodded at Brogan. "I think I'm going to call it. I'll see you for lunch tomorrow in Orange Beach."

"Good deal," Brogan nodded.

Alec said good-bye to the group and exited. It wasn't long and the rest of the group started breaking up leaving Seth, Ophelia and Marren finishing their drinks.

"What fun!" Ophelia smiled.

Marren finished, sipping through her straw, "I know it was so fun. I missed Addie but Jubileigh did a great job on the bike and was a hoot to hang out with!"

"She always is. Southern belle meets a little bit of smart ass, she's one of my favorites," Ophelia laughed. "So, I noticed you talked to Alec tonight. Any hopes of working things out?"

Marren waved her hand, "I talked to lots of boys tonight."

Ophelia nodded, "Yes, but none that you are in love with. You're still in love with Alec."

Marren shook her head, "No I'm not. I was just trying to be nice. Call a truce."

"You can say that, but I see how you still look at him. There's no denying how that boy is lovin' you. Maybe give him a talk?" Ophelia smiled warmly.

"I can't. Alec is dangerous for me. He screwed me up and I won't let that happen again. My life is just the way I want it right now, in control."

Ophelia laughed, "Girl, the best times are when things are out of control. Just think on it."

Saturday afternoon was a beautiful day for lawn work, however Marren was completely frustrated. Getting the large stump out of the backyard turned out to be more than what she bargained for. She had been at it for hours with several breaks for iced tea and a phone call to her dad for some advice on the saw she had borrowed that wasn't working. Hacking away at the stump with a large hatchet, she realized why the previous owners left the stump in the landscaping.

Her back was to him, but she heard him approach.

"You shouldn't be here, Alec. You're not very stealthy with your surveillance today," Marren said, not turning to look at him.

He walked in her backyard through the open fence. "I wasn't trying to be stealthy. I didn't want to startle you."

"I didn't give you my address, so now you're a stalker?" Marren stood upright and turned to face him.

Alec smirked, "I would call it excellent detective work. I was running and your car is in the driveway. I knew you lived just a few blocks from downtown."

"I'm busy, so hello and good-bye." Marren turned, gave him a nod, and turned back giving the stump another whack, then threw the loose pieces in the wheel barrel.

"I see that you're busy. Why don't you have a company come in and remove the stump?" Alec questioned.

Marren was pissy, "because I want to do it myself. They wanted $500 to remove the stump and I want to put that money towards the new backyard I have planned." She turned away from him, continuing to work out her annoyance by whacking the stump, "I didn't think it would be this big of a project."

"You need some help," Alec offered.

"If I can't get it myself, I'll get Max or Brogan to come over." Marren picked up the loose pieces, throwing them in the wheel barrel.

"Why would you do that when I'm here? Let me help you."

Marren turned, frustrated and sweaty. "I don't want you to help me." She blew the loose hair out of her face with a puff. "You and I need to keep things at a distance. I'm not comfortable with you being here. Like you said on Thursday, I'm seeing someone."

"You said you were dating. That is less serious than seeing someone. Plus I'm offering to remove a tree stump not sleep with you." Alec noticed the power saw on the table. "Why not use that?" He walked over to the table, picking up the saw.

Marren's face was red with heat from working and now a little anger, "Did you not hear me?"

Alec looked at her with a raised eyebrow. "I'm Addie's brother helping her friend out. Think of it that way."

Marren was annoyed but wanted the stump removed more than she wanted to argue with him. "Fine. As soon as the stump is out, so are you."

"Fine," Alec said with a little testiness to his voice.

"It won't start." Marren said about the saw.

"Is it new? Can you exchange it?"

Marren shook her head, "No. It's not mine. I borrowed it from the neighbor three doors down. He has all kinds of tools in his garage. When I asked him how to get it going he said he hadn't used it in a long time. I don't think he's ever used it, looks brand new."

Alec looked it over, "The safety is bent. Do you have a screwdriver?"

Marren nodded. She walked in the back door of the garage and returned with several sizes of flathead screwdrivers.

It wasn't long before Alec had the saw started.

"Thank you." Marren gave him a small smile.

"I'll chop it up." The saw was smaller than a chainsaw but even for him it was not a small tool to work with, the bulk and weight making it a challenge to command.

Marren looked at him, "Are you sure?"

After watching Alec lift and pull the cord to get the saw going, she was happy not to be working with the tool.

He smiled, "I'm sure."

Marren nodded, "I could get you some iced tea. And I will clean up the wood once you're done."

Alec smiled, "The tea sounds good." He went at the stump for more than an hour, stopping briefly to take a break on the patio. He was hot and sweaty. The iced tea was delicious going down his throat. "Are these your plans for the back yard?" He looked at the sketches and notes.

Marren nodded, "Yes. Most of that will be done in the spring. I wanted to get everything pulled out and ready right now so it breaks the job up a little." She put her tea on the table and walked back over to the shrubs she was cutting down and removing.

"I'll cut them down with the saw. That will save you time. You can get in with the shovel easier." Alec walked over, started the saw and took all the shrubs she wanted removed down in minutes. He went back to the stump.

Marren had been working in the yard for six hours with Alec's help for two and a half. The stump was removed, and all of the pieces put in the wheel barrel.

"I'm going to call it a day." Marren rubbed at her shoulder, walking back to the patio table for her iced tea. "I'm sure you got more than you bargained for. Thank you for your help."

Alec followed her to the patio. He took a big drink of his tea. "You're welcome." He stepped behind her, placing his hands on her shoulders. "This is awful."

Marren had two large knots in her right shoulder muscle leading up to her neck. She flinched when he took her shoulders in his hands but didn't move away.

"I think it's from whacking the stump with the hatchet."

"Let me see if I can get it. Maybe I can loosen it enough that a hot shower will help." Alec massaged and worked the knots, feeling her body relax slightly. "This backyard will be beautiful when you're done." His hands continued to massage.

"Thank you. I hope so." Marren closed her eyes, enjoying the massage.

"How are things with the house in Mobile?" Alec asked.

"The rental is good. I have nice tenants. They are never late with their rent and seem to be taking good care of it. The rent is enough that it pays that mortgage and is paying a portion of the mortgage for this house. I only have four years on the mortgage in Mobile. I'm in good shape with both properties. How was the sale of the DC condo?"

"Really good. I got the asking price, so it paid for the house here plus money in the bank. That helps with the brewery."

Marren nodded, "That's great. When do you move in?"

"I'll be in on the First of December."

Alec's thumbs moved to the middle of her back, working up to her neck and back down again. He felt her stop herself from leaning towards him. Alec swallowed, taking a moment to think before he spoke.

His voice was gentle, "When you ended things last year, I didn't know what to do. I felt so lost. I wanted to drink it away, that was my solution. I didn't want to think I just wanted to shut every thought down." Alec paused, moving his fingers to the base of her head and working her neck muscles down to her shoulders. "By Sunday night I had been hammered for three days. I was out of control. The entire weekend is remembered in bits and pieces. When I woke up Monday morning, I was embarrassed about what I had done. I apologized to her, fuck I couldn't remember what exactly was said or done. I explained I was trying to get through the weekend and drink you away. Marren, I was humiliated without you knowing and now feel sick over you knowing what I did. I hurt you because of something I did out of my mind on booze. I can't be sorry enough. You know that is not who I am. I am truly sorry that I did what I did and hurt you. More than that I'm sorry I ever let you go. I should have gotten my ass on a plane, should have done so many things different."

Marren didn't say anything. Her eyes were closed, and she was glad she wasn't facing him. She had the urge to push her face in his chest, let him hold her and take away some of the hurt she had been feeling for so long.

Alec's lips touched the crown of her head, "Forgive me, Marren. Let me spend some time with you, see if you can love me again. Think about it." Alec's hands stopped massaging and instead he gently touched her neck and shoulders. "I leave tomorrow and won't be back until the end of November. Please open the door just a little."

CHAPTER 8

Alec returned at the end of November with a moving truck. For nearly two weeks he was slammed with unpacking and meetings overseeing the brewery. Finally, ready to get out and cut lose, he attended the Bone and Barrel Christmas party that was on the second weekend in December. Everyone was attending, including Marren.

She had returned his text messages that he limited, not wanting to push her away. Her responses were friendly. Alec was happy that most of the hostility seemed to be gone.

Alec walked over to the table, smiling. He shook hands with the guys and kissed the women on the cheek, wishing everyone a Merry Christmas.

He scooped his sister in a hug, "How are you? I haven't seen you all week."

"Good. I am consulting on a couple cases for the FBI." Addison had gone private with her accounting business but still offered assistance when needed. She was one of the best forensic accountants in the country. "How's the house coming?"

"Ok. I'm in pretty good shape. Probably need more furniture. You'll have to take a look." Alec smiled taking the beer Max handed him. "Thank you." They clinked beer necks and took a drink.

"I love to spend your money. I will gladly take a look," Addison laughed.

Alec noticed Marren talking to Jared at the bar. Neither looked happy. "What's going on over there?"

"Not exactly sure. She didn't know Jared was in town. He has been in Chicago since October."

Alec joined the men but continued to watch the conversation at the bar. He couldn't tell what was said but whatever just went down wasn't good. Jared looked like he had just been punched in the stomach and Marren's face was upset. He watched Jared exit and Marren order another drink. When she approached the group of women, she forced a smile and started talking to the girls. A few hours into the night, everyone settled in seats at their table.

"Here you go. Grinch shot!" Addison was trying to give Marren another drink.

Marren frowned, "That's like my fourth one. I'm done. Stop ordering yourself a drink and making me drink it."

Addison giggled, "Come on. I want to feel like I'm still partying with you. Take one for the team."

"Are you crazy? I'm not sure what team you are on but it's not mine. You're trying to get me drunk."

Max laughed, "I don't think she's trying. You are pretty much already there."

Addison gave Max a look, "I'm just trying to help."

"No help needed," Marren laughed. "I'm good."

Addison smirked, "You didn't look too good at the bar earlier."

Alec was seated next to Max. He leaned in so he could hear the conversation.

Marren waved, "It's fine."

"That did not look fine," Addison laughed, taking a drink of her non-alcoholic cocktail.

"We talked about his traveling with work and how I'm not falling for him. Come on, I've been on, what, five dates with the guy in like four months. That conversation was ridiculous." Marren took a drink of her beer.

Addison smiled, "You told him you're not falling for him?"

"No, he told me since I'm nowhere near ready to fall in love with him he doesn't see a reason to continue dating. He thinks at four months I should know if there is potential or not." Marren rolled her eyes and took a drink of her beer. "It's not four months of dating. He hasn't been in town. Somehow he turned into the girl in this situation and I'm not expressing my feelings enough." Marren laughed, "Go figure."

Addison smiled, "What did you say?"

Marren shook her head, "Nothing. He's right. I don't have warm and fuzzy feelings about him. He's a nice guy but I barely know him. And after that conversation..." Marren shrugged.

Ophelia got up, "Come on girls, let's dance."

All the women stood up, following Ophelia to the dance floor.

"Men never do that," Max commented.

Seth laughed, "No we don't. We don't look like that either." Seth smiled, watching his wife shake it.

Max leaned towards Alec, "You going to make a move?"

"My sister is getting her drunk. I don't think there will be a move to make," Alec chuckled.

The party ended with Marren lit like a Christmas tree. She hugged Addison, "I'm going to hate you tomorrow. You know that, right?"

"But you had fun tonight! We will drive you home." Addie hugged her.

"I'll take her home," Alec offered. "I'm going by her place to get to mine."

The four walked out of the bar together. Alec put his hand on Marren's lower back, making sure she was steady on her feet. She was doing ok on her own but the sidewalk seemed to sway a bit beneath her feet.

"I'm wasted. Your sister is a horrible friend. I'm going to be hung over tomorrow." Alec opened his passenger car door, helping Marren in.

"We will get you some water and Advil before you go to sleep." He closed her car door.

Marren sat back, closing her eyes.

When Alec got in the car, he looked at her, "Are you ok?"

"I need to go home." Marren spoke softly.

Alec had only driven a block when Marren said, "I don't feel good. I'm going to be sick."

He pulled the car over. By the time she opened the car door and got out, he was already there to help her. Marren leaned over, throwing up. Alec held her hair back and steadied her by holding her shoulder. When she was done, he handed her a napkin he had grabbed when he got out of the car.

"You ok? Think we can get you home?"

Marren nodded.

As soon as Alec opened the door to Marren's house she took off for the bathroom. She was sick. Not a little sick but terrible, wrenching sick. He found a couple wash cloths and wetted them with cool water. Alec placed one on the back of her neck when he held her hair. He gave her the other to wipe her mouth. The heaving and vomiting went on for some time before Marren seemed ok enough to stand up. She brushed her teeth, used mouthwash, washed her face and put her hair in a pony-tail. Alec looked in a couple of her dresser drawers, finding a t-shirt for her to wear to bed.

"I'm sorry," Marren offered, exiting the bathroom in a t-shirt and panties.

No sooner than she made a few steps towards the bed, she turned around, running to make it to the toilet again where she spent another fifteen minutes being sick. Alec winced, feeling the pain for her. She was not good and he knew all too well how that felt.

"You're going to be ok. It can't keep going." He handed her another washcloth.

Marren was mortified, "This is so gross. I bet this is a real turn on for you. Great way to end your night."

"Were you trying to turn me on?" Alec chuckled.

Marren looked at him, "Don't make fun of me. I'm just saying this is not how I want you or anyone for that matter to think of me." She brushed her teeth and used mouthwash again.

Alec gave her a small smile; "This is not what pops in my head when I think of you." He handed her a bottle of water and some Advil. "Think you can take these without throwing up again?"

"Let's hope." Marren took the pills and a sip of the water. "Addie is in big trouble."

Alec laughed, "I'll help you get her back." He was more serious when they walked to the bed. "I'm going to stick around for a little while. Make sure you're ok."

Marren wasn't in any shape to argue. She was just happy he had pulled the blankets back. She got in bed with her head sinking in the pillow.

"The room is still spinning."

"I brought the bathroom trashcan just in case." Alec placed the can next to her on the floor. Marren was up two more times to be sick before sleep finally took over.

Alec woke to Marren partially covering his body. He had rested on the opposite side of the bed from her the night before. Fully dressed and on top of the covers, he fell asleep watching over her. At some point during the night she moved to him, resting her face on his chest with her leg over this thigh and her arm across his middle; a familiar position. Alec smiled as he held her. He had always loved the way she felt against his body. Marren was quiet when she slept causing Alec to steady his breathing, hoping to keep her asleep and next to him as long as possible.

"Mmmm," Marren moaned softly. Her hand rose to her forehead and eyes. All of a sudden, she realized she was sleeping on Alec and sat up. She looked at him almost in a squint as she held her head. "Why are you still here?" Her voice was soft but concerned.

"You were up in the middle of the night sick a couple of times. I didn't want to leave you sick like that."

Marren lay back on her pillow. "Why are you in my bed?"

"I'm fully dressed and was on this side. You came over here. Not that I minded but I was keeping my distance." Alec sat up. "How bad is your head?"

"I'm dying. My head is going to explode." Her eyes were shut.

Alec walked out of the room, returning with a bottle of water and two Advil.

"Sit up, baby." He closed his eyes, "Marren," he corrected himself, trying not to get kicked out of her house.

She sat up, taking the Advil and drinking some water. She couldn't take the upright position and lay back again.

"I'm going to make you something to eat. Let's get you in a hot shower." Alec walked to the bathroom.

"No I can't move. I'm just going to lay here and die. You should go." Marren was feeling very dramatic and downright miserable.

"You are hung over not dying. Come on you're tough. You can do this. I'll feed you and leave."

Alec started the water running in the shower and collecting clothing from her dresser drawers, he prepared everything for her.

"I'm not tough. I can't. I need to sleep through the misery. You don't need to take care of me. Call Addison, she caused this." Marren kept her eyes shut.

Alec walked over, scooping her up from the bed, "Sleeping right now won't help. A hot shower, drinking water and food will. You can sleep after and if you want Addison, call her yourself."

Marren clung to Alec, both arms around his shoulders and her face rested in the crook of his neck. She inhaled.

"I always loved the way you smelled." She was so miserable and felt she deserved this one little pleasure of smelling Alec.

He held her an extra minute before putting her on her feet.

"Do you need my help with your clothes?" Alec was hopeful.

She looked at him like he was an idiot, "No."

He kissed her forehead, "Let the hot water work it's magic." Alec left her alone to shower.

Marren was dressed in a tank top and silky pajama bottoms when she emerged from the bathroom. Her hair was soft, just blown dry and brushed. She felt a little better, but the headache was not giving up yet.

"A little better?" Alec asked, sitting on the edge of her bed. He could tell she was still not great.

"A little."

"Good. Come with me. I have some food for you."

Marren looked pitiful, "I'm not sure I can eat anything."

Alec walked to her, placing his hand on her lower back. "Just something to get you over the hump. You can't just have Advil and water in your stomach."

Marren took a few bites of the breakfast burrito Alec made her and drank a large glass of iced tea.

"I'm going back to bed. Thank you for taking care of me."

Alec cleaned the kitchen but upon hearing Marren leave the bathroom he walked in her bedroom, "Were you sick?"

Marren gave a quick smile, "No just brushed my teeth." She had never been sick around Alec and was finding his care sweet.

After cleaning the kitchen Alec walked back in Marren's bedroom. She was lying on her side. He could tell she wasn't asleep by her breathing, but her eyes were closed.

"Are you ok?"

"I think I might not die. But I'm not sure I would say ok. Are you leaving?"

Alec walked to the side of the bed and brushed her hair off her forehead.

"Do you want me to leave?"

Marren hesitated, "You can stay. It doesn't mean more than Addie's brother helping me, right?"

Alec grinned, "Maybe a little more."

"Will you stroke my hair like you used to?" Marren asked with her eyes closed.

Alec got under the covers on the other side of the bed. He was dressed in his jeans and t-shirt but he had removed the button-down shirt from the night before. This time he came to her, moving to her side of the bed. The front of his body to the back of hers, he stroked her hair.

Marren leaned back into him. "That feels good."

Alec had a smile on his lips, "It does. Your hair is so soft. It's beautiful. Your beautiful even hung over."

Marren laughed, placing her fingers against her temple, "Don't make me laugh. It hurts."

"I'm serious. The most beautiful woman I have ever met. I miss you so much, baby."

Marren turned to him, burying her face in his chest. Alec shifted to hold her to him, continuing the stroking of her hair.

"When I walked in the Christmas party, seeing you in that red dress, I couldn't take my eyes off of you. There have been a million times the way you look has stopped me in my tracks. This morning, you asleep on my chest, your face is so beautiful. I never get tired of looking at you."

"Alec." Marren's face pushed slightly deeper into his chest.

"It's true. I should have told you things like that every day when we were together. I felt them. Thought about you constantly. I thought you knew how I felt but what I was doing about moving here and my job made you doubt me, and I hate that." Alec's lips pressed against her forehead, giving her a drawn-out kiss.

He held Marren in silence, letting her relax. He continued stroking her hair for a long time until she rolled away from him. This time Marren took him with her. She held to his arm pulling it over the top of her. Alec shifted his body, pressing it firmly to her; his arm covered her with his hand on hers. They both slept for several hours.

Marren woke in Alec's arms. Lying still, feeling his warmth and weight made her feel at home. Her thoughts were that she could get lost in him again and that scared her to the point she wouldn't let it happen.

"I can feel you thinking." Alec didn't open his eyes.

Marren sighed, "We shouldn't be doing this."

"You weren't feeling well." His fingers tucked her hair behind her ear. "This is the first time I've ever been with you when you were sick. I wanted to take care of you."

Marren chuckled, "I don't get sick very often and I can't remember the last hang over like this. A slight headache is one thing; this is ridiculous."

Alec rolled her to her back, looking at her face, "You look better. Feeling better?"

She watched his lips move, wanting them and hating that she did. His hand moved, touching her waist. The tank top had shifted, exposing a little of her skin that his fingers touched. Marren nodded in response; she thought if she spoke, she would kiss him.

"Good. My work here is done." Alec gave her a half smile. He swallowed hard, wanting to take her lips but not knowing if she would refuse him. His face lowered to hers slightly. When she didn't move or turn away, he brushed his lips against hers once, then twice. That was all it took, the heat between them erupted like a volcano.

This was pure lust for Marren. Hot, angry sex was all she was willing to have with him. Her touch was demanding and fast, not leaving her time to think. She pulled and pushed at his clothing, removing her own when he removed his. Marren's mouth demanded his kisses, taking no time to breathe or savor each other's lips. Her hand covered his, guiding where she wanted to be touched and with what strength. Alec felt her bitterness towards him rolling off of her in waves. Moments of anger and forcefulness mixed with desire and what he hoped was still love. He tried to slow things down, but she wouldn't let him turn this experience into anything but sex; the type of sex that was hot and shameless with a need to get her to her orgasm.

When Alec's fingers entered her, she arched her back, moaning in a way that sounded like she hadn't been touched in a long time. She hadn't. No more than a kiss good night or a hand on her back since she broke up with Alec. Marren hadn't moved on. Her breathing was fast and winded and the sounds of soft and sexy cries coming from her lips was more than Alec could take. He moved his body between her legs.

Once he felt Marren give up her first orgasm, he wanted, needed, to be inside her. Angry or not, they both wanted each other.

Marren panicked, "Wait, wait," her hands were forceful against his chest. "I'm not on the pill anymore." She was trying to catch her breath. "Under the sink in the bathroom."

Alec got up, moving quickly. He returned next to her bed, rolling the condom on, hoping she hadn't reconsidered. Marren was still catching her breath from the foreplay when he moved between her legs, stopping short of entering her. His hand held the side of her face when his lips pressed hard against her mouth, his tongue finding hers to taste. He caressed his hand over her body on course to hold her hip, sliding over her breast and down her waist until his fingers locked on, lifting her hip slightly to take him.

Alec's erection was potent. The desire for her was immense but he knew to slow his thrust so he didn't hurt her. He pushed inside, feeling Marren's fingertips dig in to his lower back. He heard a soft whimper in her kiss. Alec backed out slightly, moving slower when he pushed deeper. He broke their kiss to look at her face.

Marren's hands grabbed his ass cheeks, pulling him in.

"Slow, baby. Slow down."

Marren heard the tenderness in his voice and closed her eyelids. Alec watched tears escape the corners of her eyes sliding down to her hair. Marren pushed her hips toward him, taking him in deeper. Her eyes opened when her head lifted from the pillow to claim his lips in a heated, hungry kiss.

Neither of them lasted any length of time before they were over the edge. Alec remained inside her for a long moment after they finished, his face nestled in her hair. He gently moved to her side, draping his arm over her. Marren wouldn't allow him to cuddle or hold her, though. The brief contact was all he received before she removed her body from his and her bed. She walked in the bathroom and closed the door behind her.

Alec heard the shower turn on. He sat on the edge of the bed for a brief moment, contemplating what would be the right move; join her, forcing an interaction, or leave her to whatever she was thinking.

Marren felt the cool air from the open door. She was facing the hot water with her eyes closed, letting it run over her, when Alec stepped in behind her.

His hands massaged her shoulders, "Talk to me."

"You can have the hot water. I'm done." Marren turned and her fingers grazed his chest when she moved around him, stepping out of the shower.

Alec walked out of the bedroom dressed in his clothes from the night before. He found Marren in the kitchen sipping tea, making grilled cheese on the stove.

"Can I feed you before you head out?"

"I guess you're booting me then?" Alec sat on a stool at the kitchen counter.

Marren paid attention to the grilled cheese. "I've taken your whole day. I appreciate you taking care of me. I'm feeling better."

Alec watched her for a few moments, "We need to talk. I've been telling you how I feel, apologizing, explaining, and you've said very little, if anything. There is still so much unsettled between us. Talk to me, Marren."

"It was sex. We don't need to talk about sex. Let's just call it what it is. We're attracted to each other. I can't deny that. I…" She was lost for her words.

Alec gave his head a shake and pushed his lips together before saying, "That's bullshit."

Marren's expression hardened when she looked at him.

He gave her the same hard look. "I know you. Granted that wasn't making love exactly but you don't just have sex. Hell, we waited six visits, enjoying long weekends and dating for three months before we slept together. You're off the pill. There hasn't been anyone since me, has there? I know you are angry with me but you still have feelings for me. You don't have sex that doesn't mean something."

"But you did!" Marren could feel the heat come to her face. "I don't want to have feelings for you. When I think about another woman touching you or you touching her I feel sick over it." Marren's eyes filled with tears. "I can't get lost in you and let you hurt me again." She wiped at the tears that leaked on her cheeks.

Alec stood, his voice direct. "I will never hurt you again." He moved towards her, but she put her hand up letting him know to stop. "Marren, when I think of what I did, it makes me sick. I can't change it. If I could I would. I'm begging you to forgive me." When Marren didn't respond Alec's voice turned gentle, "You haven't moved on. You could have but you didn't. Give me another chance. I'll never be ok without you. You are the one. Please find a way to work this out with me." Alec took her in his arms even though she had warned him off. He held her to him, feeling her rigid in his embrace. "I love you. Come back to me." Alec kissed her forehead before leaving her home.

CHAPTER 9

"**M**ax will be over at 3pm to help with the food," Addison said, moving her yoga position.

Marren whispered, "Perfect. Drinks and appetizers are at 4pm. When will his parents be in town, tomorrow?"

"Yes, they are coming in tomorrow. Neither of them were working on the 23rd so that was perfect and they didn't have to travel on Christmas Eve. Thank you for hosting all of us for Christmas Eve."

"Thank you for hosting me and my parents on Christmas. My mom and dad are flying in tomorrow as well," Marren smiled.

"Alec is wondering how you are feeling about him coming over on Christmas Eve," Addison inquired.

Marren nodded, "Alec is welcome. My parents love Alec. They won't give him a hard time. I kept what went on between us private."

The yoga instructor eyed all of the women as she walked by them.

Addie whispered, "Drill Sergeant Yoga."

Marren smiled, "Be nice."

"Why do your parents think you and Alec are not together?" Addison inquired.

"Work. Geography. That's not the whole story but a good part of it."

Addie nodded, "I'm looking forward to seeing your parents. They are so much fun."

Marren laughed, "They are now. Try growing up with an army colonel."

"Are you coming for beer and burgers tonight?"

"No. I'm grocery shopping and I need to finish decorating. I have my classes tomorrow night. Surprisingly, people want to beat each other up before Christmas," Marren raised an eyebrow.

Addie laughed, "That doesn't surprise me. Sometimes good defense moves are needed for a family holiday."

Marren was finishing up with the high school girls when she noticed Alec walk in and take a seat on the benches. She instructed two classes on Thursday evenings at the Fairhope Rec Center. Both were mostly self-defense but the adult class that followed the teen class offered Krav Maga, which included some combat moves.

"Ok ladies, show me the hold and counter again."

Marren walked around the sixteen girls that were paired off. One girl was the attacker and the other the victim. She had them running drills of being grabbed by the arm and how to get away.

"Good. Everyone looks good. Bring it in for questions." Marren watched the girls walk to her, forming a semi-circle. "How does everyone feel tonight about the lessons?"

The general consensus was that the girls were excited about the new techniques they used.

"Ms. Marren, what if someone is so much stronger you can't break their hold?" Hillary, a junior, asked.

Marren frowned, "It's not a matter of being stronger. You have to out think the other person. Move quickly. Be three steps ahead. We are never looking to fight a larger person, we are looking to get away. Just because someone is stronger, doesn't mean they are smarter or as fast as you." Marren looked at Hillary, "Can you show me an example of how a stronger person's hold would make you think that you can't get away?"

Hillary walked up to Marren shyly.

Marren nodded encouraging her, "Show me what seems scary to try to get out of."

Hillary put both hands on Marren's neck. Marren rotated bringing her arm around, elbow breaking the hold and ready to attack.

"See what I did?"

Hillary nodded.

"You try it." Marren placed her hands on Hillary's neck and instructed her how to pivot, turn and break the hold with her elbow.

"Good." Marren turned back to the group, "What's the rule ladies? We counter until we are free and we?"

"Flee!" the girls shouted.

"Excellent. Ok. Our time is up. Everyone have a happy New Year. See you in two weeks." Marren waited for a moment and called, "Hillary."

Hillary walked over to Marren.

"Hey pretty girl. What's going on?" Marren asked.

Hillary shrugged, "I don't know. Probably nothing. I got in an argument with the guy I'm dating; he's just really strong. He was in a fight last week with a guy over something stupid. I'm not sure about him because he's really angry some of the time."

Marren nodded, "You break up with boys like that. If you're not sure and you don't feel safe, you don't date him. Right?"

Hillary nodded, looking down.

Marren touched her chin for her to look up. "You don't take any nonsense. Good men make you feel safe. Break up with him if you don't feel safe with him."

Hillary gave her a half smile, "Ok."

Marren smiled, "Ok. Have a nice Christmas vacation."

"I will. You too." Hillary hugged Marren, who returned the hug.

Marren looked at Alec who stood, walking toward her.

"What are you doing here?" Marren raised an eyebrow.

"You are really good with the girls," Alec smiled.

Marren smiled, "Thank you. They're all getting pretty good or at least more confident." Marren looked at him dressed in work-out clothes. "You didn't answer me. What are you doing here?"

"I'm here for your next class," he smiled.

Marren shook her head, "No way, Jacobs. Go workout with your muscle junkies."

Alec laughed, "Muscle junkies? I thought you liked my muscles?" His eyebrow lifted flirtatiously.

Marren ignored him, "My class is mostly women."

"I already signed up and paid my money. You're stuck with me. And you have two men in the class besides me."

Marren shook her head, "This is a beginners Krav Maga. You already know these techniques. And nobody looks like you in this class."

"I need a refresher. Plus I wanted to talk to you about your parents and this weekend." Alec's voice was quiet and serious.

Marren gave him a look of sarcasm, "A refresher?" She shook her head in disbelief. "You'll be fine with my parents; they love you. They don't know anything besides we couldn't get the living in different states worked out."

Alec nodded, "You didn't talk to them?"

Marren shrugged, "I talked to them a little but our problems were private. Same reason I didn't talk to your sister. What should I have said? I don't want everyone involved in my love life."

Alec sighed touching her arm, "You were hurting and you didn't talk to anyone. I hurt you and you kept it to yourself. Marren, I'm so sorry."

Marren knew what he was getting at. The reason she was still as upset as she was a year later was that she never dealt with it.

Marren stepped back, "And who did you share your feelings with? I don't think you took out a billboard."

"No, I didn't shout things from the roof tops but I did share how miserable I was with Max and my sister. I left you message after message. I tried to deal with losing you. I got a plan to get my ass here and fight for you."

Marren looked at him, "What are you trying to do? Get me upset before my class?"

"No, I want you to talk to me. Say everything you have thought or felt. Get it out so we can deal with it. I want you back, I want to move forward, and we can't do that unless you can let go and forgive me." Alec watched her wring her hands nervously. "I deserve the eruptions of anger so lay it all on me. Don't say some smart-ass comment, get upset and freeze up. Let me have it if that's what you need to do."

Marren's students started walking in, joining her and Alec on the large practice mat. Marren opened the class with pleasantries and answered questions about the previous class. She walked everyone through demonstrating the previous lesson before talking about what they would work on during the current class.

"We are going to work on a new position. I need a volunteer to help me demonstrate a headlock situation." Marren looked at the group of twenty.

Nobody volunteered. She smiled, "I'm not that scary, come on."

"We want the big guy to do it." Sophie Bryant a woman in her late fifties suggested with a smile.

"Sure." Alec stepped forward with a cocky smile.

Marren was not pleased. She and Alec did not work out or train together. They would run that was the extent of their workouts. Nothing that ever resembled rough housing, self-defense or combat moves were part of their relationship.

"Are we sure we want the new guy? Maybe let him observe since it is his first day?" Marren offered.

"We want the new guy." Another woman in her late forties cat-called with a whistle.

Marren chuckled, "Ok. This is Alec."

Marren smirked when she heard the women say, "Hi Alec," in a sweet song. She had Alec step up, showed him how to grab her and followed up with the instruction of breaking the hold and attacking him. All done in very slow motion as she explained each move.

"Here we have Alec holding me in a common headlock." She hesitated, letting everyone see the hold. "I'm going to step toward him, giving him the idea that he has the control and momentum." Marren bent over in the headlock and stepped forward. "Doing this I'm throwing my weight on him giving him more to balance, moving with him. Right away I will strike towards the groin." Marren showed the movement of striking him but didn't make contact. "He will focus on this hand, trying to stop the attack. My other hand is moving around to the hair or the nose, both vulnerable areas." Marren demonstrated. "I'm going to push him up and away, bringing my other hand up to hammer fist in the neck area and push him away." Marren demonstrated each move slowly without making contact with the punches.

Alec was not surprised by Marren's strength or technique. He had heard from his sister what she was capable of and knew of her reputation with the FBI. He had never tested Marren's fighting abilities; he wanted to make love to her and that was his physical interest. Holding her in a way that was aggressive was uncomfortable and played with his head a little.

Marren positioned them again, "Alec is going to hold the headlock tight as he would if he was using it on the street, not here in class." She looked at him. Knowing he was not comfortable, she encouraged him to do the hold properly.

Alec smiled nervously, "I think you should have one of the girls help with the demonstration."

Sophie Bryant spoke up, "She won't hurt you sweetie. At least not that bad."

Sophie and a few others snickered.

Marren smiled at her students, "Be nice." She looked at Alec with a smirk, "You volunteered."

Alec's arm held her in the headlock tight. Marren moved quickly, showing all of the moves she had demonstrated slowly. Alec had been pushed away with ease. She made contact with the attack strikes but nothing to hurt him, it was just to get him off and away.

"Ok everyone pair up and choose who is going to be the attacker for the first drill." Marren stepped back from Alec. She almost laughed when Sophie Bryant took Alec by the hand, saying he was with her.

The class ran the drill a dozen times before Marren demonstrated another hold and counter. By the time the class was over everyone had two moves to practice before sessions would resume after the first of the year.

Alec hung back waiting for everyone to leave. This time when he approached, he took her gym bag to carry for her. "I'll walk you to your car."

Marren scoffed, "Hopefully just to be chivalrous. I think it's pretty clear I'm not in any danger." She smiled.

"Yes, to be a gentleman. We've never done that before. Sparred or tested each other's techniques. I wasn't comfortable doing that with you." Alec walked next to Marren. "That's not how I want to touch you." His hand stroked her hair gently, brushing over her back.

Marren nodded. "How was Sophie Bryant?" she teased with a giggle.

Alec tapped her on the bottom, "Very funny. She's divorced. Three dogs. Looking for love and invited me to her Bay House for a crab and lobster lunch."

Marren couldn't help but grin and laugh, "Mmm. Sounds good. I bet she has something special planned for dessert."

"I told her I was hot for the teacher. She'll have to get her dessert elsewhere." Alec shook his head with a laugh.

They reached Marren's car. He put her bag in the trunk and walked over, standing in front of her at the car door. He put his hands on her shoulders.

"I was half expecting you to make a few of those punches count when you were demonstrating with me."

Marren's eyes met his, "I would never hit you out of anger or to hurt you."

Alec pressed his forehead to hers, "Will you go out to dinner with me?"

"You're eating dinner at my house tomorrow," Marren responded.

"On a date. Will you go on a date?"

Marren shook her head, "Not a good idea."

"It's a great idea. We can start over."

Marren pulled away, "Start over? How do you propose we do that? How do we forget more than two years?"

"We don't. But we start again. Look, I know we can't pick up where we left off, but we can start again. Move on from where we are right now."

Marren looked at him, "That would be me being vulnerable. I would have to let you in and that means you having the ability to break my heart. No. I already did that." Marren shook her head. "You have no idea how I felt. I wanted you so much but you were so stubborn about us. It all had to be on your timeline and what was good for you. I don't think you ever loved me the way I loved you. And now you're here and I should just give you whatever you want? What about what I wanted for a year and a half? You knew what I wanted and you..." Marren looked down and stopped speaking.

"I what?" Alec wanted her to get it out.

"You took me for granted. I was so in love with you, you knew I would just wait, I would put up with not being together for the holidays, you not putting me first. I would turn myself inside out to be with you. Well I won't do that now."

Alec gave his head a shake, "I loved you exactly the way you loved me." Alec took her face in his hand, "Exactly. I hated being away from you. I knew what you wanted, to get married, have a family. You don't think I wanted that?" Alec searched her eyes. "I want that. I needed to be able to provide for you. I couldn't move here without a career that would support a wife and children. I have money in the bank, but I wanted to make sure you had everything. I needed to be able to take care of you for the long haul. I was putting you first even if it didn't seem like it. Marren, I'm sorry that you felt I was taking you for granted." He watched Marren close her eyes so she didn't have to look at him anymore. "You have the ability to break my heart. I will turn myself inside out to be with you. You are first." His lips touched hers, "You were always first. I've wanted you for my life since we started dating."

He felt Marren's fingers clench his t-shirt at his waist. Alec kissed her cheek and her forehead, "You're everything."

Alec's kisses moved back to her lips. Marren didn't resist his kiss. His mouth explored hers gently, nibbling and tasting her lips, his tongue conveying the message of wanting her. "Come home with me. Let me make love to you."

"My parents are at my house. I have to go." Marren took a step back.

Alec nodded. He closed the distance between them, taking her in his arms again, "At least tell me you will see me after Christmas, lunch, dinner… something?"

"I want to think about it," Marren whispered.

Better than a no, Alec thought. He kissed her again, wrapping his arms around her. He felt encouraged that she held on to him.

CHAPTER 10

"I can't wait to see Addie and that little baby bump," Rayna Quinn smiled while helping her daughter prep food in the kitchen.

Marren gave a little laugh, "She's really cute. In her head the bump is much larger than it is."

"She has such a small frame I bet 10lbs is going to be a lot of weight for her, let alone the normal twenty-five or thirty. Is she over the morning sickness?"

"Yes. Max is feeding her everything in sight. Speaking of Max, he should be over anytime to help with these appetizers. Keep stirring that, we don't want it to stick. He's a kitchen Nazi!"

Mrs. Quinn laughed, "I've been cooking long before all you were born. Don't boss me in your kitchen. Are you nervous or something?"

"I just want dinner with everyone to be nice. This is my first Christmas in this house and I want it to be perfect. What do you think of the decorations? Too much?"

"Darling, your home is gorgeous. Out of a magazine beautiful. Relax. Have a glass of wine; I think you need one. I have a feeling you're more nervous about a certain boy coming to dinner?"

Marren scoffed, "First I'm thirty-five. Boys were long ago and I'm not nervous about Alec. Why would I be?"

Mrs. Quinn raised an eyebrow, "Because you don't know what your dad is going to say to him."

Marren stopped peeling the shrimp and looked up, "There's nothing to say to Alec. This is a friend and family holiday. We are not going to put Alec in the hot seat. Why would he say anything?"

"Oh I don't know; you're his daughter. Alec did something that broke the two of you up. Now he's in Fairhope. Maybe curiosity has the best of your father?"

"We didn't live in the same city. That's enough to break anyone up. Mom, I'm serious. I don't want anyone uncomfortable. It's Christmas." Marren was talking fast.

Mrs. Quinn smiled, "Mmm hmm. You're not nervous at all."

The doorbell rang.

"I'm serious Mom. Please go warn your husband to be nice." Marren washed and dried her hands, walking out of the kitchen to the door.

Colonel Fitzgerald Quinn opened the door to Max and Alec, who were carrying bags and pans of food that Max had prepared for the family dinner.

"Gentlemen, merry Christmas." Colonel Quinn greeted them, taking a portion of the load Max was carrying.

"Merry Christmas, Sir." Max smiled. "Thank you for the help."

"Is there more?" Colonel Quinn asked.

"Yes, Alec and I can run back out." Max moved past the Colonel, letting Alec move forward.

"Merry Christmas, sir. How was your flight?" Alec smiled, unable to offer him his hand to shake because they were full.

"Very good, son. I hear you're in Fairhope full time. Congratulations on the brewery and new position with Mobile PD."

"Thank you. I'm getting settled in. It's only been a month in my house. I start with SWAT January 2nd." Alec walked in the kitchen with the Colonel.

"Alec, sweetheart. It's so good to see you." Mrs. Quinn walked over, hugging him. "Merry Christmas."

"Merry Christmas, ma'am." Alec reciprocated the hug.

He looked at Marren, giving her a smile, "Merry Christmas. I'll help Max bring in the rest of the food and I can clean those. I know you don't like to."

Marren smiled, "Oh, thank God." She laughed. "It is a merry Christmas."

Marren laughed, washing her hands and squeezing lemon on them to get rid of the shrimp smell. Cleaning any seafood was her least favorite thing to do in the kitchen.

The group of Alec, Max, Marren and her parents gathered in the kitchen talking while Max and Marren prepared appetizers. Alec had cleaned the shrimp and was looking for something else to do. He felt anxious around her parents, unsure if they held any resentment towards him because of the breakup. He wanted to get things out in the open. If they needed to say their piece, he hoped they would do so immediately.

Colonel Quinn spoke up, "So Alec, what do you think about this program my daughter is spear heading with the Mobile PD? I'm not happy about it."

Marren rolled her eyes, "Great lead." She laughed, "You can't ask someone's opinion and include yours so they agree with you."

"I can. I don't want my daughter working with cops on the take. The lines get blurred as to what team everyone is on. You're walking into an ambush."

Marren looked at her mother for help.

"Fitz, lighten up. This isn't the Army. Nobody is ambushing any-one. Get yourself a beer." Mrs. Quinn smiled at her husband with a warning in her eyes.

"Sir, I'm not up to speed on the program. I only know a portion of what is planned. I took the position with the knowledge we would be working with a special team. The goal is to remove the problems we have on the force and train the department to use tactics that are not lethal when working with suspects. I don't see Marren walking into an-ything but training." Alec tried to calm the unease Marren's father was feeling.

Marren swallowed.

Colonel Quinn shook his head, "You haven't heard the latest. The FBI will be helping you clean up Mobile PD. They are not just training, they are helping IA nail and remove the problems. She's going to be involved in the clean-up."

Alec looked at her. "When did that happen?"

"It's Christmas Eve. We can talk about work next week. Turn up the Christmas music and everyone please get something to drink." Mar-ren looked at her mother.

"Alec, sweetheart, will you get me a glass of red wine and let's have a chat. I would love to know what has been going on between you and my daughter." Mrs. Quinn smiled at Marren.

"Mom!"

Alec smiled, "Of course. Cab or Malbec?"

"Malbec." Mrs. Quinn walked out of the kitchen.

Marren looked at Alec, "I already told her we are friends. Every-thing between us is fine."

One corner of Alec's mouth turned up. He held two glasses of wine as he walked towards Marren.

Alec kissed her on the cheek, "We're not just friends. If you were my daughter, I would have a conversation too. I knew they would talk to me today, that's why I came over early with Max. It's going to be ok."

Mrs. Quinn kissed Alec on the cheek after they were done talking. "You're a good man Alec. I'll keep my fingers crossed for you."

No sooner than Mrs. Quinn left the sitting room, the Colonel arrived with two beers.

He handed one to Alec, "So you broke her heart and now you're trying to win her back? Not that she would tell us, but I figured since she wouldn't speak your name..."

"Yes sir." Alec nodded sitting up straight. "I hurt her and I'm trying to figure out how to make it right between us.

Colonel Quinn looked at him for a long moment without any expression. He took a drink of his beer.

"Son, my daughter is amazing. She is tough on the outside with the most beautiful heart. You're going to be lucky if she lets you anywhere near her heart again." Colonel Quinn leaned back on the couch, taking another drink of his beer. "You have your work cut out for you."

Alec relaxed slightly, "I know. I'm going to do whatever it takes to get her back. I love her and my intention is to marry her."

Colonel Quinn smirked, "Has she agreed to date you again?"

Alec smiled, "Not yet."

The Colonel nodded, "All of the romantic things you did with my daughter, they were never lost on her. She called her mother, talked about you like she had found what she had always wanted."

Alec's face turned serious, "I want to be that man for her."

"So we're on the same page," the Colonel hesitated, "don't fuck up again. You have my blessing if she takes you back." He stood, offering Alec his hand to shake.

Alec stood shaking his hand, "I won't, sir. Thank you."

They returned to the kitchen at the same time Addison and Max's parents arrived. Alec walked over to Marren, who had wide eyes, concerned about the conversations.

He stepped behind her spoke softly in her ear, "No worries." He kissed her cheek.

The dinner was full of great conversation and excitement for the new year. The food was delicious with both Max and Marren receiving praise. Addison loved the attention she received about her pregnancy, with Max teasing about doubling their grocery bill. Both families had a genuine rapport with one another, finding it easy to be together.

"We've had so much fun. I'm looking forward to tomorrow." Max's mom spoke to Marren's mother while they helped clear dishes. Marren walked in the kitchen, "Moms, I'm going to handle the clean-up. Please go relax with a glass of wine. Mom, please keep Dad from discussing my job with everyone. He's on it again."

"I heard that." Marren's dad said, walking in the kitchen. "You will be working with men Alec's size that are not happy to be getting direction from you. Re-think this. Cleaning up drugs and money with cops on the take is not what you signed up for."

"Dad, I'm smart about work. Don't under estimate me." Marren dismissed his concerns.

Mrs. Quinn smiled, "Come on Fitz, let's finish the evening with a glass of wine by the fire. The parents are going to leave the children to clean up." Marren's mother gave her a wink.

Marren sat on the couch with her feet on the coffee table and a glass of wine in her hand. Alec sat in the same position, a little space between them.

"Good day."

Marren smiled with a nod, "It was. Thank you for staying and helping with the dishes." She took a sip of wine, "What did my parents say to you?"

"Nothing terrible. They were both concerned, wanting to know what is happening between us now." Alec sipped his wine.

"What did you tell them?"

"I want you back. I'll never hurt you again. My intentions."

Marren looked at him, concerned, "I'm sorry. I didn't want them putting you on the spot."

Alec smirked, "I deserved it. You are their baby and the only girl. I understand them being protective."

"My dad is losing it over my work." Marren took a drink of her wine.

Alec didn't say anything.

Marren glanced at him, "You agree with my dad?"

"I didn't say that. I'm not sure. I want to evaluate the situation. The last thing I want is for you to be in danger. I know you are good at what you do. I have no doubt you can handle yourself. Working with you is going to be hard for me. Being in your class, running that drill was difficult for me."

"We won't run drills, you and me." Marren sipped her wine, turning toward him.

"I don't want anyone running a drill with you, especially SWAT. I'll be out of my mind to see someone touch you like that."

Marren touched his arm, "I'm more than capable. Please don't worry."

Alec turned to her, "We'll see."

"I don't have a date for New Year's Eve. You asked about taking me out after Christmas," Marren changed the subject.

His fingers touched her cheek, "I would love to be your date."

Marren nodded, "I made plans to go to dinner and the tent party with our friends. I'm sure you did too. We can go together."

"Anything you want." Alec moved his face closer, wanting to kiss her.

Marren looked at Alec's lips and raked her teeth against her lower lip. She tilted her face, offering her mouth to him. Alec's lips were tender when he kissed her.

He spoke softly between kisses, "You look so beautiful. Your dress, your hair, my God baby, you are so gorgeous."

Alec put his wine glass on the coffee table, taking her glass doing the same. His next kiss was passionate as his hands held her body to his. Marren wrapped her arms around his neck, kissing him with passion. Long kisses caused Alec's hands to wander over her. Her breasts were felt over her dress with his thumb strumming the fabric that pushed from her aroused nipple. Marren sighed into the kiss that was lighting them both on fire.

His hand moved to the hem of her dress, sliding under and grasping her thigh, "I want to touch you."

Marren's head fell back slightly in a sigh when his hand touched her inner thigh. Feeling his hand move between her legs, her lips went back to his with a fiery kiss. His fingers stroked her center over her panties and she heard herself moan softly in the kiss.

`Her lips broke away, "I love when you touch me." Her face raked down his neck as she said the words.

Alec's fingers continued to seduce her sweet spot until she was ripe for an orgasm. His thumb took over the strumming when his fingers slid inside her. When her head fell back, he took full advantage of kissing her neck.

"I'm going to taste you. You have to stay quiet."

Marren nodded, breathing heavy. Alec knelt on the floor in front of the couch. His hands slid her panties down her legs, removing them. He pushed her dress up and putting his hands on her hips, he pulled her forward so he could bury his face between her legs. A long, gentle lick with his tongue made her lurch towards him.

Alec whispered, "You are so sweet."

His tongue and teeth went to work. Her body trembled in his hands. Marren felt the tingle and exhaled with a soft whimper. Alec stopped.

Speaking quietly with a smile he warned her, "Shhh. You have to be quiet."

Marren nodded and Alec continued with his mouth on her. She kept her moaning under control until his lips sucked her in. A sexy whimper and "Oh God!" couldn't be stopped.

Alec replaced his mouth with the soft touch of his fingers. He sat on the couch, pulling her to him with his free hand.

His mouth kissed her briefly and he whispered, "Your parents are going to know I'm doing dirty things to you."

"I can't help it. I tried to be quiet." Her whisper was broken with raspy breaths.

His lips covered hers again briefly. "I want to make you come but you have to be quiet."

Marren gave a slight nod. Alec continued to kiss her, his mouth absorbing her soft moans while he finished her off with his fingers.

Christmas Day was fun at the Ross home. Marren arrived early to help with dinner and to give presents to Addison, Max and Alec. Addison and Max went first. They opened a box full of children's books to read to the baby they were expecting. Marren had picked each book specifically for Mom or Dad. Max's books were about food, fishing or the ocean; his favorite things. Addie pulled out books about math, birthday cake and stories of courageous characters.

"These are great!" Addison hugged Marren.

"I'm glad you like them. I wanted to get your bookshelf started." Marren was happy with her choice of gift.

"That is yours. It's from all of us." Marren was talking to Alec, pointing to a four-foot wrapped gift tucked behind the Christmas tree.

Max walked over to help pull the large gift out. Alec unwrapped a beautiful painting for his home. It was one he admired at Jubileigh's gallery.

"No way! This is the one I was looking at," Alec smiled.

"We know. Marren saw you looking at it and asked Jubileigh about it. Heaven knows you need something on your walls," Addie smiled.

"I just moved in." He gave his sister a look. Alec looked back at the painting, "This is perfect. I love it. Thank you all for doing this."

Alec picked up a pretty wrapped box and handed it to Marren, "This is from all of us."

Marren opened the box to a string of outdoor lights and a picture of a beautiful arched garden pergola. She looked up at Alec.

"Is that the right one? From the magazine you were looking at when we cut the stump out?" Alec smiled, hoping he was right.

Marren nodded, "Yes but this is really expensive. You guys can't do this."

Addie smiled, "We already did. Alec shopped around and found a company in Daphne that is coming to install it as soon as you set a date."

Marren hugged all of them thank you with her hold on Alec lasting a bit longer than Max and Addison's.

Addison turned, winking at Max who was following her to the kitchen, "Did you notice something has changed between them the last couple days?"

Max nodded, "Yes, I've been less worried about Marren pulling her gun," he laughed.

"Very funny. I want to ask her what's going on but I don't want to spook her."

"Do not ask her. Listen chatty Addie, you don't need to know everything that goes on with everyone." Max took her in his arms.

Addison kissed Max, "But I do." She laughed snuggling to him. "How long until we eat?"

Max laughed whispering in her ear, "This pregnancy has been about sex and food and you needing one or the other. As soon as we have this baby, I'm getting you pregnant again."

Addison laughed, "No you're not!"

Alec opened his car door for Marren, he had offered to take her home after the Christmas festivities ended. She stayed to help clean the kitchen when her parents returned to her house. Max and Addison lived five blocks from Marren, with Alec living three blocks from her.

Alec started the car as he spoke, "I love getting both of our families together. It makes me think about my parents and how they would have enjoyed the holidays with everyone." He started to drive.

"I would have loved to have met them," Marren smiled, looking at Alec.

"They would have loved you. My mom, you, your mom and Addie with your quick wit and smart mouths would have been fun. My dad would have enjoyed conversations with your dad about the military. I'm sure they would have argued Army or Navy but still there would be good stories." Alec's father was a Navy Seal before he was a Boston, Massachusetts police officer.

"When you left the Army did you choose police work because of your dad?"

Alec shrugged, "Maybe, but mostly because it seemed to fit. Why the FBI?"

"I grew up with three older brothers and my Dad. They were always shooting targets or beating up on each other." She laughed. I was the girliest tom boy there was. My brothers would cringe when I walked outside in pink dresses wanting to shoot guns. My dad showed me how to shoot and that was it. I was a better shot than the boys."

"Why the FBI still?"

Marren looked at him raising an eyebrow, "My dad is working on you. More talk about the Mobile clean up? I like teaching what I know. I'm a great instructor and I love it."

"I think so too. So just instruct. Don't do the investigation part of the task force."

Marren shook her head; "We are going to see what comes of things before I decide what is good for me. He's got you spooked. Last night you were worried about me instructing and now tonight you're worried about me investigating. Stop." Marren touched his hand. "I'm a great agent. I know my job."

Alec nodded pulling up in front of her house. He put the car in park. Reaching over, he unfastened both of their seat belts and immediately took her in his arms. The kiss was needy and rushed. His hand grasped the nape of her neck, holding her firmly so his mouth could get carried away. Alec's lips and tongue made love to her mouth so possessively that Marren could only think of wanting them everywhere. Winded, she broke the kiss, only to have Alec's lips run down her neck to the places that gave her chills.

"Make love to me, Alec."

His mouth kissed hers again, gentle but quick. He drove the three blocks to his house, parking in the driveway.

"Are you going to give me the tour?" Marren asked as they walked inside.

Alec picked her up, wrapping her legs around his waist and began walking to his bedroom.

Between kisses he said, "It's just a house."

Alec placed Marren on the bed, helping to remove her clothes in the midst of passionate kisses. His lips kissed over her body, finding their destination between her legs. Tonight, she didn't have to be quiet. Tonight, he would do things to make sure she couldn't be quiet. Alec had managed to shed his clothing while enjoying Marren. When her second orgasm left her winded and collapsed on the bed in satisfaction, Alec kissed up her stomach to her breasts.

His voice crooned, "How do you want me, baby?" His tongue tickled over to her neck, "I want to make you feel good. What do you want?"

Marren turned her face to kiss him, "Any way you want. You can have me any way you want."

Alec made quick work of rolling on a condom and moving between her legs. Eyes glued to hers, he pushed slowly. Marren's neck arched and she sighed in a way that made him feel at home inside her. When her eyes focused back on his, she lifted her face, needing his kiss. Alec braced his body to hover over her so he could watch the effect he had on her. She was beautiful, writhing off the bed to meet his body, causing him to go deeper. Too much of a good thing was bringing him to the edge so he backed off, only to feel her push towards him harder and faster.

"I'm going to come," she notified him in a raspy voice.

Marren bit her lower lip until his lips pressed against hers. Her fingertips dug into his lower back and shoulder when he felt her tighten around him. It was all he could do not to follow her.

When he felt the last wave of her undoing, he rolled her to her stomach. Lifting her hips, he pushed inside, hammering away at her until she cried his name in the way he had always loved to hear. The sound of her voice finished him.

Afterwards they held each other, letting their bodies relax and their breathing return to normal before Marren sat up.

She looked at him and smiled, "Dear God, Jacobs, I feel like I ran five miles." She giggled, "Sad part is, you did all the work."

Alec sat up kissing her shoulder, "Stay."

"You know I can't. My parents are at my house." Marren smiled. "But I want to."

"Ok. How about I stay with you?"

Marren shook her head with a smirk, "You want to see the Colonel at 5am and explain what you were doing to his daughter?"

"I can sneak out. I want to sleep with you on my chest. I'm not ready to be without you." Alec kissed across her shoulder.

"You are taking me on a date soon. I'm not going anywhere. My parents are visiting so we'll have to wait. Plus this isn't exactly taking it slow." Marren gave his lips a quick kiss and hopped up to get dressed.

CHAPTER 11

Marren's parents visited until New Year's Eve morning when Marren dropped them off at the airport. They enjoyed their week, just the two of them during the day while Marren worked. When Marren returned home after her workday, plans were made for all of them to go to dinner or drinks with Marren's friends. Alec found excuses to call and invited the Quinn's out frequently so that he was included in the majority of their plans. He couldn't get much time alone with Marren, with the exception of walking each other to the car to say good night. Almost a week of only kissing and hugging was building a need for her that was so intense he figured he would explode when he touched her.

"Hi." Marren smiled wide as she opened the door on New Year's Eve.

Alec smiled, "Hi. You're alone right?" He offered a beautiful bouquet of flowers to her.

"Were you hoping my parents decided to stay another week?" Marren pressed her lips together, stopping a smile.

Alec wrapped his arms around her with a hand palming her butt cheek, "No I was not. I love them but I need you." His mouth covered hers in a kiss that made her weak in the knees.

"I need to put these in water." Marren walked in the kitchen, pulling a vase from the cabinet. "They are beautiful. Thank you."

"You're welcome."

Alec watched her fuss with arranging the flowers. She was dressed in black pants that fit her perfectly and standing on high heels that gave her another two inches. His favorite was her black silky shirt; it was an off-one-shoulder style with a tied closure on top of the other shoulder. He wanted to untie the shirt with his teeth. She looked beyond sexy. Her hair was down and wavy, and she wore beautiful make-up with glossy lips. Alec felt his cock getting worked up in his jeans.

"We can get a drink at the bar before everyone meets for dinner." Marren looked at her watch as she walked towards the couch to get her jacket. "We have time."

Alec watched her ass move and shook his head.

"You look gorgeous. I don't want to mess you up but take your pants off."

Marren turned to look at him. Alec had hunger in his eyes as he stripped off his sports coat.

When he unfastened his belt, she smiled. "No drinks?"

"No drinks." Alec slipped his shoes off, continuing his approach.

Marren moved around to the front of the couch, sliding her pants off. She watched him stare at the tiny thong she had on before she removed it. She removed the silk blouse for good measure, leaving her standing in a black lacy strapless bra and sexy high heeled shoes. "Sit on the couch, Alec."

He smiled, enjoying that she was taking charge. He removed his pants and boxer briefs, keeping one of the condoms he had in his pocket. When he sat down, he tore the wrapper with his teeth and rolled the condom down over him. Without a touch from her, he was rock hard just from looking and thinking about how amazing it would feel to be inside her. Marren climbed over, straddling him. Her lips gently kissed him before her teeth grazed his lower lip. She slowly slid down his length, taking him in deep. Alec's head fell back on the couch. When Marren started rocking and riding, his hands held on to her ass cheeks.

"You're so hard. Do I feel good?" She kissed his neck and then her teeth took his earlobe, giving it a gentle rake and tug.

"You feel so fucking good. Slow down though." Alec's breath caught, "I've needed you for days, I won't last."

Marren kissed his lips then his neck. Her voice was raspy and seductive, "Nobody ever touches you but me. Only me." Marren didn't slow her pace, instead her bottom lifted and lowered with such intensity and speed that he moaned with enjoyment. Alec's arm wrapped around her, holding her in place while his orgasm raged; his face buried in her breasts.

Marren stroked his hair and she whispered, "I love you, Alec. I always have, always will."

His face lifted to look at her and she brought her lips to his. The kiss was an acknowledgement that she was forgiving and moving forward.

CHAPTER 12

The women, Addison, Paisley, Jubileigh, Marren and Ophelia sat at a high-top table at Bone and Barrel enjoying beer and burgers after Wednesday night yoga in early February. All of their significant others were training staff at Brew and Burger Fairhope. The grand opening was scheduled for Friday and the staff were prepared, but the men scheduled a mandatory final training to go over every detail, from prepping food to taking guest orders. Friday night's performance needed to be flawless.

"Seth is so tired. He is grummmmmmpy! Livy told him, 'Turn that frown upside down' this morning." Ophelia giggled, "I don't think he liked that she repeated his saying and used it on him." Olivia was four years old and the spitting image of her mother. Ophelia took a drink of her beer. "I don't blame him. Between teaching, this place and the brewery, sleep hasn't been high on the list of priorities. Our girls are missing their daddy, so is mommy." Ophelia pouted her lip.

Paisley smiled, "I hear you. Miller hasn't been able to lighten his hospital schedule so he's working fourteen hour days and his days off are long at the brewery."

"We are all in the same boat. Brogan hasn't had a full day off since we got back from Key West after New Years'. He's testy when he gets home and completely in work mode before he leaves the house in the morning. I'm looking forward to the grand opening and the manager's taking charge," Jubileigh added.

Addison laughed, "Max told me it would be helpful if I learned how to cook just a little." She put her hands on her baby bump. "I told him I have something in the oven so he should feed me. I guess making him omelets for dinner three days this week didn't make him happy." Addison shrugged. "It was that or carry-out."

Marren laughed, "You are spoiled." She threw her napkin at Addison.

The other women laughed doing the same.

"I can't help it. Would you want my experimental, hoping for the best cooking or would you want Max to cook for you?" Addison giggled. "All I've wanted to do during this entire pregnancy is eat and have sex. The man is definitely over worked but I have needs." Addison wiggled her eyebrows. "Seriously though, I've set up all the accounting for the brewery and payroll system. They are all set for credit card processing and the tax accounts with the state. The ordering system is going to be great for inventory. This is the same system Max is using at The Pillars. I've been trying to help with what I can do best. He should want to feed me," Addison giggled again.

Ophelia smiled, "I noticed Marren hasn't said Alec is grumpy." One eyebrow lifted with a fun grin.

Marren shook her head, "No, he's been good."

Addison rolled her eyes, "They are on the love and sex high. They don't need any sleep right now. I asked Alec how he was juggling SWAT and the brewery," she took a sip of her iced tea, "he said 'Everything is good as long as I'm home with Marren every night.'"

"Awwww," all the women sang, looking at Marren. Her cheeks blushed.

"So which house is going on the market?" Paisley asked.

Marren shook her head, "We haven't moved in together. Just staying at each other's place depending on schedules."

"Have you talked about it?" Paisley asked.

"No." Marren shook her head a little. "It's too soon. I don't want Alec spooked. I mean we just got back together two months ago and before the break up we were only seeing each other once a month. I don't want him to feel like I'm smothering him, we see each other almost every day, but moving in…" She shrugged, "I doubt he's ready for anything like that."

Addison choked on her iced tea. "My brother said the same thing about you. He's worried you will try to slow things down if he speeds them up."

Ophelia laughed, "Y'all need to get married already." She raised her glass. All the ladies joined, looking at Marren.

Marren smiled closing her eyes with a little shake of her head. Then she raised her glass, giving the other glasses a clink.

Marren walked in Alec's house on Thursday night after her Krav Maga classes at the Rec Center.

"I'm home," she announced.

"Bedroom," Alec answered.

Marren slipped off her gym shoes at the door and took a bottle of water out of the refrigerator before heading into Alec's bedroom. Her eyes were wide as she saw the room from the doorway.

A big smile spread across her face, "What is all this?"

The room was lit with candles. Soft music played. The bed was turned down. Alec sat on the edge of the bed in boxers. He looked so damn handsome.

"Come here," Alec smiled.

"I..." Marren looked down. She had on a gray FBI t-shirt and yoga pants. "Let me take a shower. I want to look pretty. I …"

Alec stood and took her hand. "You look pretty. You are beautiful all dolled up or in workout clothes." Alec brought her to the bed, sitting back down. Marren stood between his legs, "But my favorite is when you don't have any clothes on at all." Alec stripped Marren out of her clothes. His eyes roamed her body taking in her shape, "You are perfect." His lips kissed her neck. "I love the way your hair smells, like lavender and you."

Marren's body pressed towards him as his hands ran down her back. "I thought you would be exhausted and nervous with the opening tomorrow." Her fingers raked his hair.

Alec kissed down her shoulder, "Nope. We're ready."

His hand cupped her breast, readying it for his mouth to suckle.

Marren's head fell back, "I love that."

"I know. I know everything you love."

Alec's free hand slid down the curve of her waist to her hip. His thumb brushed the sweet spot between her legs. He heard Marren sigh. Looking up, he watched her bite her lower lip.

"Let me have those lips," he requested.

Marren's face moved, offering her mouth to Alec. His kiss was so much that she was jumping out of her skin. His tongue danced, his lips were firm and then soft. The man kissed her a million times and a million times she was done for. She heard the soft pleading noise from her throat. He knew exactly what to do to her and how to do it.

Alec's lips left hers to trace down her neck. "I want to be inside you. Watching you come."

Marren moaned softly from his words, from his thumb circling and teasing, and from the thought of him pushing deep inside.

"I want that too."

Alec moved back on the bed, removing his boxers. He lay flat on his back with a pillow propped under his head.

His hand reached for hers, "Come here baby."

Marren got on the bed, kneeling next to him. He opened a condom and rolled it on. Alec watched Marren straddle him while he lined himself up to be mounted. Marren slowly lowered, taking every inch with a soft sound catching on her exhale. Her eyes met his and she leaned forward to kiss him.

"No baby. Stay up there. I want to watch you." Alec held her hands, putting them on her thighs. "Show me how good I make you feel." He thrust his hips up, encouraging her to move.

Marren circled, grinding down on him. His cock was so hard and deep that her breath caught when she circled to the right and he brushed against the spot inside her that stopped time. She moved around again and again, working herself towards her goal. Her hands clenched on her thighs as she felt Alec's hold over her hands tighten.

"Let me touch you," Marren moaned. Her eyes were wild as she moved on him. He only allowed her to touch him through their connection.

"You got this baby. I can feel how close you are. Fuck, you are so beautiful. Come for me, Marren."

Marren's eyes closed and her head tipped back slightly. Her body rode him as if she were galloping on a horse with harder and harder descending motions. Feeling every inch and the impact sent her over the edge.

"Oh God, Alec!" She cried.

Alec watched in awe. The build up, climax and her coming down was a movie he would play over and over in his head. He flipped her on her back, never leaving her body.

Marren was still catching her breath when he looked down, smiling at her. "You are amazing. You do it for me. Everything about you." Alec kissed her lips. "I love you. I had no idea what being in love was until you. I am yours. I always will be."

Marren's hand cupped his cheek, "I love you and I'm yours. I've never felt this way about anyone or anything. I don't ever want to be without you."

"I promise you, you'll never be without me. I can't be without you." Alec kissed her over and over, making love to her.

All hands were on deck for Brew and Burger Fairhope's grand opening. All the women, all the men and the brewery's staff were making the night a huge success. From the ribbon cutting by the mayor to the final burger delivered to the last customer, everything went as planned. Everyone was dead on his or her feet. Beers were poured for the group of ten, while Addison drank root beer. All raised their glasses in celebration when the doors locked for the night.

Marren walked naked to her bed, where Alec was already under the sheet waiting for her. She smiled at him, thinking he was hot. He was on his side, head held up on his hand with a bent elbow. His free hand brushed across the mattress, summoning her to lie next to him.

Marren got in facing him, "It was a perfect night. I'm so proud of you."

"Thank you." Alec rolled her on her back, his leg between hers with his body partially covering hers. "Perfect is right here. When my body is touching yours, that's perfect. It's home."

Marren giggled, "Your home is between my legs? I like it, but don't tell anyone if they ask for your address."

Alec kissed her nose and laughed, "I need to think of an address for this."

Alec climbed over her leg with his body settling between her thighs. He brushed her hair from her face.

"You are so beautiful. I love you so much. I finally know exactly what my dad had with my mom." Alec swallowed hard. "He worshipped her. Thought she was the one that hung the moon. I never quite understood that. But now, I get it. I am so grateful that I get to feel this way."

Marren's eyes filled with tears, "Alec." Her voice was a whisper; her hands touched his neck and shoulders gently.

Alec's lips brushed hers, "Marry me, Marren? I need you every minute of every day."

Tears spilled from the corners of her eyes.

She nodded, "Yes." Her smile was beautiful. "Yes." She pulled him to her, hugging him around the neck. "I love you. I love you, Alec."

He pulled back from the embrace. Lifting off her, he took the ring that he had been holding and placed it on her finger. Alec kissed the palm of her hand. Marren's eyes grew large as she looked at her engagement ring.

She pushed up on the bed in a sitting position, "Alec, it's beautiful."

He smiled, "I was hoping you would like it. Let me tell you about it." He moved next to her, bringing her to his chest. "This diamond was picked out just for you." Alec's finger pointed to the center two-carat marquise diamond. "These diamonds were in my mom's wedding ring." Alec referenced the three diamonds on each side of the center stone. The diamonds were beautiful baguette diamonds. The setting was done in platinum with a wide band.

Marren looked up at him, "You gave me your mom's diamonds." Her eyes spilled over with tears.

"Yes, baby. They were given to me for my wife." Alec's hand touched her face wiping the tears. He kissed her forehead. "We are getting married. That means you're my wife," he teased.

Marren nodded, "I love my ring. Thank you." Her voice was happy, with a sentimental sob entwined.

"Thank you for saying yes. So when can we get married? I was thinking next weekend."

Marren laughed, "Next weekend?"

Alec shrugged, "Why wait? What do we need? Our family and friends, your dress, a tux for me? We can pull that off in a week."

Marren snuggled in his neck. "No, we can't pull that off in a week. I want a beautiful dress and my brothers will have to put in for leave. Plus, don't you think you are a little tied up with a new brewery and a brand new job?"

Alec took Marren's face in his hand, "You can have anything you want for the wedding: beautiful dress, flowers all the things you've thought about. I just don't want to wait a long time. I messed up missing out on time with you when I was living in DC. You are most important, not the brewery, not my job."

"Ok. What about this summer? That's only four months away. Maybe end of June or beginning of July? That gives me time to plan and my brothers can get leave."

Alec nodded, "Where? Do you want to go home?"

Marren shook her head, "This is our home. I want to get married in Fairhope. What if we do it under the pergola, all lit up? The backyard will be done by then. We could do the whole thing, tent with air conditioning, dance floor in the backyard."

"Sounds perfect. So…" Alec smiled, "since we are negotiating, I want to move into one house, yours. We can either sell mine or have another rental property. I want to move in now, not in late June or July. Since you won't marry me next weekend, I think I should get to move in next weekend."

Marren giggled, "Oh you do?"

Alec flipped her on her back, taking up residency between her thighs, "Yes I do. Give me what I want."

He started kissing down her body with his mouth crashing on the sweet spot between her legs. His licks and tickles were teasing. He heard Marren moan.

He paused for a moment "So, is that a yes?"

Marren's head pushed into the pillow, "You can have anything you want."

Alec grinned for a moment before continuing with his tongue.

Alec had agreed to keep their engagement on the down low for the rest of the weekend. Everyone was excited about the brewery and Marren didn't want to distract from that. Marren teased that his sister would start making wedding plans immediately, so best to focus on the brewery. They decided that the Wednesday night yoga, beer and burgers get together would be a perfect time to make the announcement.

Marren stretched and took the first position on the yoga mat. She was waiting for one of her friends to notice the rock on her finger, but they managed to get through twenty minutes of yoga positions and talk about the brewery opening before Jubileigh noticed.

"Holy moly that man loves you!" Jubileigh moved to Marren's mat, grabbing her hand. "When did he do it?"

All the girls stopped talking and looked over. Each moved quickly to Marren's yoga mat.

"Friday night. We decided to wait and tell everyone tonight." Marren was giddy happy. "He said the sweetest things and oh my God, I love that man."

All five women hugged each other with Marren being in the center. They giggled and said congratulations with each friend taking Marren's hand and giving compliments on the ring.

"Ladies, take it outside." The yoga instructor stood before them with her arms crossed.

They all giggled, rolled up their mats and walked out to the parking lot where they continued to carry on with hugs, questions and plans to celebrate in non-yoga attire.

"Bone and Barrel for champagne!" Ophelia announced.

Addison followed Marren to her car and gave her a hug. "I'm so happy." She looked at Marren's ring, "He did a beautiful job. My mom would be so happy you are wearing her diamonds." Marren hugged Addison tight, both women crying. Addie pulled away, "We are officially going to be sisters!"

Alec walked in Bone and Barrel, meeting the rest of the men. He was the last to arrive after hitting traffic driving home from work. The guys were talking sales figures and minor changes they wanted to make to the brewery when Alec walked over to join them. He sat down and was immediately greeted by the server who handed him a beer. All of the men were looking at him when he took a drink.

Alec smiled, "She said yes."

"Good run." Marren started walking, letting her breathing slow. She and Alec were at the end of their street on Sunday evening. The weekend had been busy with the brewery and moving Alec into the house that would now be theirs.

She continued, "I'm pretty tired and ready for a shower."

Alec nodded, "It's been a busy weekend. I'm all moved in. Our first night living in one house, what do you think?"

Marren took off running, "I'm getting the hot water first!" She turned, sticking her tongue out.

Alec laughed, "I don't think so." He took off after her, scooping her up and throwing her over his shoulder. "We shower together."

Marren's fingers stroked Alec's hair, his head resting on her chest after a long session of making love.

"I wish we had one more day off." Marren looked at the clock; it was after 10pm. She would be getting up for work at 6am.

"I work twelve hours tomorrow. What do you want to do for dinner?" Alec asked.

Marren smiled, "I'll be home before you. I'll make dinner. We start working together tomorrow. You haven't said much about it."

"I have mixed feelings about it. I love that I get to see you but of course I can't act like I know you. I'm looking forward to getting the bureau's training, but I don't want you working with some of the operators." Alec kissed her breast.

"You agreed in our meeting last week with the captain that it was best that your team does not know about us or your connection with the FBI. It will be better all around that nobody knows you played a role in constructing the program. If someone is going to sound off, they will do it in front of you because you are one of them. Some of the SWAT operators are going to be a problem. We know that going in. They need to be removed from the team. If they are so bad, how did they get on?"

Alec answered, "No idea. There are three hot heads that would never have qualified in DC. I'm not working with them every day because of my dual role and scheduling but a case is being built to remove them. IA is on task. I can barely keep my hands off of you, so acting like you are just another agent from the bureau and not mine is going to be difficult."

Marren thought for a moment, "Promise me that you are going to let me do my job. I've worked with a ton of men and sometimes they are not thrilled I'm the trainer. Let me handle things my way. I'll be yours as soon as you get home."

Alec looked up at her, "That is why I have mixed feelings. You do realize it is my job to protect you."

"Yes, at home. At work I'm an agent. A well trained agent that can protect herself."

Alec moved to her side, kissing her lips, "I'm not thrilled about this."

"I train men every day. It will be fine."

CHAPTER 13

Monday afternoon sixteen SWAT team members along with their lieutenant, Alec Jacobs, entered the police department briefing room. FBI Special Agent Quinn and Agent Matthews met the team. Alec gave both Marren and Tim a nod, walking to the lectern to speak. He addressed his team, going over the ninety-day training the FBI would be conducting along with psychological testing and physical evaluations. There was a rumbling of hushed voices in the group, unhappy with the feds coming in.

"This is coming down from the police chief who is working closely with the mayor and FBI. The record of this department is not a good one. If you were clean with the handling of suspects, we wouldn't be here." Alec responded to an unhappy comment.

"Our training rivals the FBI's. What can they possibly teach us that we don't know?" was a comment blurted out by one of the SWAT operators.

Alec raised an eyebrow, "How to use it." He let that hang in the air for a few moments. "Look men, you will participate. You will do exactly what this training program requires of you or you can exit to your left and be re-assigned." Alec held up a large folder, "I have a notebook of grievances." He emphasized, "Excessive force, handling of evidence, unwarranted surveillance; I can go on, but you know why you're here.

We need to clean up our act. Every law enforcement agency across this country is being watched closely by its citizens. Everything we do needs to be one hundred percent by the book. The FBI is going to help get us there." Alec went on for ten minutes describing the specifics for the week.

"Special Agent Quinn and Agent Matthews will be leading this program. I'm going to turn it over to them."

Marren walked to the lectern. She looked all business with her hair pulled back in a knot at the nape of her neck, navy blue FBI t-shirt, khaki fatigue pants with pockets, military style boots, and her badge around her neck. She heard hushed catcalls from a few of the men. Marren was beautiful and her uniform couldn't hide it. She ignored the testosterone in the room as she had done on many occasions over the eight years she had been working for the FBI.

"Good afternoon. I'm Special Agent Quinn. Agent Matthews is handing out a quick evaluation that each of you will need to fill out. This is a mini psych eval from Quantico for new recruits. It will give us a brief glimpse of where you are mentally in regards to your job here in the department. While he's handing this out, I will share with you my work at the bureau and how I got here." Marren talked about her eight years with the FBI, honors, promotions, high profile cases she'd worked on, programs she trained and/or participated in, weapons mastery, hostage negotiation and finally closing with her most recent work. It was obvious that she had far exceeded the sixteen team members in training and expertise.

"In the last twelve months, I have lead training programs like this one with our field offices across the country. Our focus for this program is how *not* to escalate a situation, how *not* to take a life. It is our goal to train on how to get the best results for everyone involved and that includes the perpetrator. While that is our goal, we will also go through weapon and firearms training along with hand to hand combat training. Mid program we will talk about hostage negotiation. We are here to help, give you new techniques and improve on the techniques you already know. Our goal is to leave you with new strategies, maneuvers, and better weapons handling so that you are serving our citizens in the best way you can." Marren paused, "Once you have your evaluation completed, we will head over to the gym for the physical evaluation." She nodded, "Any questions?"

"Yeah doll, what's your first name?" Officer Martin snickered.

Marren gave a half smile, "You may call me Agent Quinn or Quinn. I'll call you Operator Martin or Martin."

"Figured we should be on a first name basis if we are going to the gym to roll around on the mat together." Martin chuckled. Several of the other men snickered.

Marren smiled, "I don't roll around on the mat. There is no together on the mat, if you end up on the mat, it will be because I put you there with force. Let's get your evaluation done, Martin."

"Martin, she is your superior and she deserves your respect. Mouth shut and get your evaluation complete instead of clowning." Alec barked from his seat.

Tim looked at Marren, not pleased with the disrespect so early in the day. She lifted her eyebrows at him, acknowledging the class clown. They knew they would get some resistance from the group. She purposely did not look at Alec but knew he was steaming pissed. This was exactly what he was not looking forward to dealing with.

Alec sat to the side of the men, listening to Marren. She was impressive. Most everything she talked about he knew, with the exception of a few of the training programs and awards from early in her career. She was humble and never boasted about her Master's in Psychological Studies from James Madison in Harrisonburg, Virginia. Alec knew that was where the FBI came to recruit her. He held back the smile that wanted to form in complete pride. She was beautiful, brilliant, loving and going to be his wife. When a couple of the men whispered comments about her, he ignored it. That was to be expected, she was beautiful and even in the t-shirt and fatigues it was obvious Marren's body had all the features men admired. When Martin was disrespectful, Alec could feel the vein in his neck throb, but Marren handled him. He remembered to breathe, trying to separate his fiancé from the federal agent standing in front of his team.

In the gym the men were given timed evaluations that were recorded. The evaluations were given three at a time with Marren, Tim and Alec recording results. Marren heard some of the comments about her body and how some of the men would like to evaluate her, but she didn't engage.

Martin scored higher than all of his team members on all of the physical evaluations. Alec scored better than Martin with the exception of the bench press. The two were comparable in size, though Martin was more bulky in the arms while Alec was defined, and Alec had height on him. Alec, even though he was the lieutenant, decided to go through the exact same training as his team so they would hopefully follow his lead.

"Lieutenant, you need to hit the weights," Martin teased.

Alec nodded, keeping it light, "And you need to run more so you can get some of that beer and those buffalo wings burned off."

The guys laughed light heartedly.

Marren and Tim spoke briefly and agreed to break the team into two with Tim taking Martin and Thomas – two of the operators that were brought to their attention as possible issues. Alec would work with Tim's group, keeping the potential problems in his sights. They set up the two groups, forming two circles and ran through holds and releases for the next hour. Both Marren and Tim showed different ways to hold a suspect with new and unique takedowns that would cause the least amount of harm to a suspect.

Alec continued to get more and more annoyed with Martin. The officer kept looking behind him, watching Marren, commenting on her body. When it was Martin's turn to pair off, Tim had to interrupt his ogling to get his attention. With ease, Martin went through the maneuvers with another officer and returned to the outer circle. Alec watched Martin and the cockiness oozing from him. Martin had ten years on the job and was popular with the guys for the mere fact he told great stories of women chasing, drinking and arrests. As time went on, Alec tried put Martin out of his mind and focus on the rest of the group, making sure everyone was mastering the new techniques. The drills lasted well into the afternoon.

Marren felt the large arms come around her in a bear hug. It wasn't tight, just powerful.

"What about this hold? How do you get out of this Agent Quinn?" Martin said for everyone to hear.

He held Quinn against him, more teasing than fighting.

Marren, annoyed, tapped his arm, "You are sparing with your teammates. Get back to your group." She tapped his arm again.

"Martin!" Alec's voice boomed.

When Alec started to walk towards them, Tim grabbed his arm, "No."

"Come on doll. Let me see what you've got." Martin gave her a goofy laugh, showing off in front of the guys.

She tapped his arm again, "Martin, remove your arms."

Martin smirked, tightening his hold and moving for a chokehold around her neck. The other men stood, watching the two, Marren and Martin on full display.

"Don't do it, Martin. Release." Marren tapped his arm.

Martin continued tightening and bringing his arms up for a choke-hold. Marren could feel his strength. Before his arms tightened to the point he would render her unconscious, Marren's foot wrapped around his leg and she used her right hand over her left fist to force and hammer her elbow into his ribs. Martin stammered back slightly and received a blow to the neck and a knee to the groin, putting him on the mat. Marren forced him face down with her knee in his spine. Martin was gasping for air due to the neck blow and she wrenched his arm behind his back, causing him to sound off in pain. Marren reached in her pocket for a zip tie and clenched his wrists behind him.

"Let's get on the same page," Marren said, her knee still pressed in his back. She bent forward, placing her forearm on his neck and speaking in his ear. Her tone was angry as everyone listened. "I'm a federal agent, mother fucker. I'm not here for your entertainment." She patted his arm, "This is universal for release. You were taught that at the police academy. Coming back to you now?" She waited for him to respond and when he didn't, she dug her knee in.

"Yes," Martin answered, out of breath.

"Good. I want to make sure you know who is in charge and it's not you. Got it?" Marren waited.

"Yes."

Marren stood, hands on her hips with Martin still face down before her on the mat, "Anyone else want to go for it? See if you can take down…" she paused, giving an emphasis on her next words, "what have you been calling me? Hot stuff." She looked at the operators.

Nobody stepped forward.

"Good. Let's get back to work."

Alec walked in the house to the smell of dinner.

"I made stuffed pork chops with roasted cauliflower. Do you want a beer or iced tea?" Marren smiled, looking at the angry look on his face. "You don't like pork chops?"

Alec stepped in front of her and taking her chin in his hand, he lifted her face to examine her neck. He looked at a slight bruise at her collarbone.

"I'm going to kill that fucker. This is exactly why I don't want you doing this. These guys are out of control. He's going to push it and I'm going to hurt him. Let us clean up our own fucking mess. Mobile has let these cowboys run the show for so long, it's going to take a miracle to get them in line. That's probably not going to happen, they will finally fuck up enough that IA can make a case to prosecute or they will be fired." Alec's fingers ran down her neck, "Nobody touches you like this. Why did you give him a chance? You should have dropped him as soon as he put his arms around you."

Marren looked at him, "Kiss me hello."

Alec looked in her eyes for a moment, the blue calming him. His lips were gentle on hers. Marren wrapped her arms around his neck. Kissing him back with her tongue dancing across his lower lip, she could feel him letting work go just a little.

When the kiss ended, she smiled, "I'm starving."

It was after 8pm and she had waited to eat with him.

Alec nodded, "iced tea. I'll get it. Do you want the same?"

Marren smiled with a nod. She dished up their dinner and placed it on the end of the island where two kitchen stools were waiting for them.

Dinner was delicious and she talked about the schedule for the landscaping that would be done in the next two weeks. What she received in return from Alec in conversation were nods and "Mmm hmm."

"Did you like dinner?" Marren asked, rinsing the dishes for the dishwasher.

"It was delicious. Thank you for cooking."

Alec knew he was being moody. He was upset about her work and couldn't get past it.

"I'm going dress shopping with Addie tomorrow after work, you'll be on your own for dinner. Your sister needs to eat every twenty minutes so we will get dinner while we're out." Marren smiled, looking at her ring.

"I returned her call on my way home. Max and Addie want to have an engagement dinner for us at The Pillars and invite everyone. If we schedule it in a couple weeks, think your parents will come?"

"They would love to but do you think we should keep it as just friends?" Marren asked.

"It's what we want. I would like them to be included as much as they want to be, if you are good with that."

Marren felt a little ache in her heart for Alec. She knew from conversations that he missed his parents, especially when it came to big milestones. Walking Addison down the aisle was an honor for him but the absence of their parents was heartbreaking for both he and his sister.

"I'm good. Just making sure you are. My parents are eager to see us. Mom was ready to buy plane tickets when we called them about getting engaged. It's perfect if they come because if I find a dress before the dinner, my mom can see it."

Alec nodded, "I'll call the colonel and see when they can make it. I'm going to take a shower and look over the schedules for the brewery."

Marren watched him walk in their bedroom. He was still grumpy about the day.

Alec sat up in bed using his laptop to go over sales figures and schedules. Marren walked out of the bathroom naked and fresh out of the shower, her hair down and silky from just being dried and brushed. Alec was still simmering over the day and tried not to look up. Out of the corner of his eye he watched her walk to the dresser and closet, getting clothes out for the next day.

"I talked to your dad. They will be here two weeks from Friday. I gave Addison and Max the date. The dinner will be that Sunday." He didn't look up, continuing to focus on his laptop screen. "I told him that they will have the other house to themselves so they can stay as long as they want. He was looking forward to it. He'll get with your mom and figure out how long they can get away. I'm excited to take them to the brewery. He asked me about going to the gun range to do some shooting while he's here."

Marren smiled. Her parents loved Alec and treated him like he was their own.

"That will be perfect. My mom will want to get involved in wedding plans." Marren walked to his side of the bed, causing Alec to look at her. "Are you done with all that?" She referenced his laptop and paperwork on the bed.

"I'm upset with you." Alec looked in her eyes, trying to stop himself from looking over her beautiful body.

Marren tilted her head to the side and placed her hand on his thigh, feeling the muscles, "How upset?" She gave him a pretty smile.

"Very." Alec's voice was stern. "Why did you let him choke you? You didn't have to let it go that far. You had plenty of time to break that hold. You tapped out three times. He should have been on his ass as soon as he grabbed you."

Marren got on the bed, straddling Alec's thighs. She picked up his laptop, closed it and moved the papers away, placing everything to the side. Her hands touched his washboard stomach.

She sighed, "The group needed to see that he could be taken down and hurt by administering a chokehold. If I would have knocked him on his ass when he gave me the little bear hug, nobody would have thought much of that, which means at some point in the next ninety days they would test me again." Her hands ran up Alec's chest. "Alec, what I did will make them all think twice about messing with me. He's the biggest guy and he needed to go down. I needed to make sure me putting him down was justified, that's why I let it go that far. Now they will all get down to business and stop looking at my ass." Marren leaned forward, placing her lips on his shoulder.

Alec took her shoulders in his hands, gently pushing her back so she would look at him, "He hurt you and it scared you. I could see it."

"I was more concerned than scared. He's strong, very strong. I knew I would be in trouble if he got a good chokehold on me. I also knew Tim would have stepped in. We've been working together a long time and he knows when to step in and how to do it so it doesn't take away my authority. You can't step in Alec. Tim told me he stopped you. These guys needed to test me today, to see how far they can push. It's a psychological game right now. The sexual comments, name calling, who is the alpha, it's all to set up to show who is in command, all intimidation tactics. Please baby, let me do my job."

Alec knew Marren was right, but he didn't like it.

"I don't want you hurt. These guys are juicing, I'm sure of it. Look, you can't expect me to just let them…"

Marren put her fingers on his lips, "Nobody is going to do anything to me that I don't allow. You watched me. I could have taken him down multiple times. I had control of that situation. I let him think he did to prove my point. You are not letting anyone and I'm not letting anyone hurt me." Marren kissed Alec's lips gently, "No more work."

Alec made love to Marren, pulling her to rest on his chest after sexy orgasms.

"I love you, baby. If anything would ever happen to you, I would go crazy. I need you Marren, and I can't have you in a position that you could get hurt in."

Marren lifted her face enough to kiss his chest, "I've been doing this job for eight years. You are just seeing it up close right now. I'm not in a position to get hurt. These are the jobs we chose. What if I didn't want you to be in danger? Your job can be dangerous, but you keep yourself safe." Her hand smoothed over his chest and abdomen, "Talk to me about something else before we go to sleep. Something sweet."

Alec smiled. She was all girl, regardless of her career choice.

"You know looking at me with those blue eyes gets you anything you want."

Marren smiled, "They do?"

Alec gave a chuckle, turning to face her and looking in her eyes.

"Yes. And you know that." He kissed the tip of her nose.

Marren nodded, "I made an appointment with the doctor to go back on the pill so we don't have to keep using condoms." Her hand ran up his chest. "I want to feel just you."

"Don't do that." Alec's voice was sweet. "At least not before we talk about kids. Maybe we just use the condoms until the wedding and take our chances after. Let what happens happen."

Marren's eyes opened wider to his, "Are you ready for that?"

Alec's shoulders gave a small shrug, "I was thinking so, yes. Are you?"

"I want a baby with you. I want everything with you." Marren's lips smiled before crashing on his mouth.

CHAPTER 14

"That one is pretty." Addison smiled. "But I think the other one is more spectacular."

Marren looked at herself in the mirror, "This is like the eighth dress here and second bridal shop. What if I don't find one?"

Addison giggled, "Uh you wear your birthday suit." She rolled her eyes, "Come on Mar, you are going to find the perfect dress. You know when you know. Keep trying them on. Just have fun. We can do this a few times. Plus, your mom will be in town and we have to try dresses with her." Addison pointed to the dressing room for Marren to try another dress.

Marren spoke behind the door, "I want your brother's jaw to drop when I walk in. None of these dresses make me think that will be his reaction."

Addison smiled, "Uh my brother's jaw drops when you walk in with a t-shirt and shorts on. You are going to be gorgeous. The right dress is out there. Trust me, you just know as soon as you put it on."

Marren took a few minutes and walked out of the dressing room in her own dress and heels.

"What about the other dress?"

Marren shook her head, "Nope. I knew when I started putting it on. Plus I'm starving. Let's get dinner."

Addison smiled, "I'm ready." She ran her hand over her baby bump, "so is the baby."

The women sat at a table for two at Kitchen on George located in a neighborhood of the Oakleigh Garden Historic District. They shared duck confit egg rolls for an appetizer. Marren enjoyed a glass of wine and Addison was happy with sparkling water served with lime in a wine glass.

"I like when they accommodate the preggo in the party," Addie smiled, raising her glass to toast. "To a beautiful bride finding a beautiful dress."

Marren smiled, "Thank you. I hope you're right."

"I'm right. First you will be beautiful, gorgeous in anything, but the right dress is out there. We just have to find it."

Marren took a sip of her wine and nodded, "Can I talk to you about something but keep it just between us for now?"

"Of course. I promise." Addison put her glass on the table.

Marren knew that if Addison promised, someone could torture her and she would never tell. Addison loved to talk and share but never if you asked her not to be discreet.

"Your brother and I talked about starting a family sooner than later. Maybe just roll the dice after the wedding and when I get pregnant, I get pregnant."

Addison's face lit up. "I want to be an aunt! Yes." She pumped her fist.

Marren laughed, "Not today. I'm talking after the wedding." Her face turned serious, "I'm not sure about work. I love what I do but being pregnant, I won't be able to do some of my job. And raising a family, we both can't do what we are doing. One of us needs to have a job where bullets don't fly."

Addison nodded, "Have you talked to Alec about that?"

Marren shook her head, "No, not yet. We just talked about me not going back on the pill and not using any birth control after the wedding. Last year I looked into a career change when I thought about moving to DC to be with Alec. My undergrad is in education. I could teach. I put some feelers out last year and I think I would like to pursue a teaching job, either high school or community college. I love working with the girls in my teen self-defense class. I feel like I could really do some good. I could use my degrees teaching psychology."

Addison smiled, "You are a wonderful instructor, so patient. I mean how long did you work with me on some of those Krav Maga moves?" Addison giggled. "And you do want to teach, your face lit up when you were talking about it."

Marren nodded.

"So why haven't you told Alec?" Addison asked.

"He's really bent out of shape about this joint task force. I don't want to get ahead of myself. If I tell him what I'm thinking, he'll want me to quit today." Marren chuckled. "I don't want to quit today. I want to make a change after we get married. Maybe in the fall semester if I get hired. I'll talk to Alec about it. I just wanted to say it out loud to someone and hear what it sounded like before I decided for sure. I know the bureau would accommodate me in a classroom setting while I was pregnant but I don't know that the FBI would be right for us as a family."

Addison nodded, "Yep. You're right Alec is uptight about the task force, especially about the officer you had to put on the mat. I talked to him on his way home last night; he was upset about it. I told him to talk to you. I also told him you did what I would have done. You handled yourself and the situation the way it should have been handled. Alec sees you as his girlfriend, fiancé," Addie winked. "He thinks you should be protected. You're his and he doesn't want anything to happen to you."

"I know. This is hard on him. Hearing about my job and what I do is one thing. Seeing it in action is something different. He sees the girly side of me out of work, he doesn't see me as an agent; at least not an agent that conducts combat training with men his size." Marren took a sip of her wine.

Addison smiled, "Well, you are wearing a pretty dress and heels. Most people wouldn't think of you as an ass kicker." She laughed and then became serious. "Alec respects your job. He is so proud of you. I love hearing him talk about how smart you are and all of your accomplishments. He sees you, all of you. I just don't think he wants anyone touching you to hurt you. You can't blame him for that. I don't know a man that would be ok with watching someone try to hurt their girl."

"I know." Marren swallowed her sip of wine. "I want to make a career change, especially when we have a family. It would be good for all of us. Summers off, fewer hours out of the house; I could work around our children and school."

CHAPTER 15

Tim and Marren stood on the field discussing the scores of the SWAT team members. The morning was spent at the FBI range for weapons training. Demonstrations of rubber bullets, shots to stop and wound instead of kill, were the goal for the exercise.

"Martin, what the fuck is wrong with this guy? It's the second week of training and I'm already sick of his bullshit." Tim commented, looking at his score. "Kill shot every time."

Marren nodded, "There is definitely something brewing among the men. Any idea? I didn't have an opportunity to talk with Alec before the exercises began."

Tim nodded taking a sip of his water bottle, "Martin had a brutality complaint over the weekend. There was a heated exchange between him and Nelson this morning, Alec had to intervene."

Marren raised her eyebrows, "Fail him on this exercise. Have him demonstrate for the rest of us what the objective was today so we can re-score him. It's better if it comes from you."

Tim nodded, "It's better if it comes from Alec. I'll take the scores to him and let him have it out with Martin. I've already had my fill of him this week."

Alec walked over to Martin, who was entertaining his merry followers.

"Martin, after lunch we are going to have you demo for us so you can be re-scored. No kill shots."

"Fuck that. Let the girlie demo. This expertise comes at a price," Martin chuckled.

Alec raised his eyebrow with a sneer. "You are going to demo. This isn't a democracy. You failed the exercise this morning, so that girlie again has out-scored and out shot you. You're dead fucking last. If you don't pass this training, you are out on your ass. So your so called expertise does come at a price, you won't have a job." Alec barked, giving Martin a look that begged for him to defy his orders. "Lunch." Alec announced to the group. "You have forty-five minutes."

Alec was exhausted of Martin but more so from the constant worry he felt for Marren working with the men. Martin and Thomas had tested Marren to the edge of misconduct all week. Alec was ready to put them both in their places. It was taking everything he had and the promise he made to Marren not to step to her defense.

Only twenty minutes into lunch Marren and Tim received notification of a hostage situation at the courthouse. SWAT received the same notification and all parties readied themselves, leaving the FBI campus.

FBI agents were on the scene with local PD. SWAT was briefed for tactical positioning along with the FBI, who were taking point. Marren was briefed and her supervisor requested that she open up negotiation dialogue. The hostage taker was a male in his early forties in a custody fight for his two small children. The ex-wife petitioned to relocate out of state for employment and was granted the request. The father had taken the bailiff's gun and was holding it to his own head. The courtroom was full with at the minimum sixty individuals. The cameras that they threaded under the door and from the ceiling and the courtroom cameras had a few blind spots.

Marren dialed the cell phone number that was provided by the hostage taker's mother who was standing by in case they could use her to speak to her son.

"Hello."

Marren could see on the camera that Kevin Jenkins held the phone to his ear with his left hand and the gun to his temple with his right hand.

"Kevin. This is Agent Quinn. How are you doing in there? Can I get you anything?" Marren spoke in a pleasant and steady voice.

"No." Kevin closed his eyes. "I mean you can get my kids back. My ex-wife cheats and now gets to take my kids. The court system is a fucking joke."

Marren took a deep breath, "This sounds like it can be worked out. You are getting a bad deal. Let's get you in front of a new judge to review what is happening. What you're doing right now isn't going to help, talking and working the problem will."

Marren waited for a response but received silence. On the camera she could see a steady stream of tears flow down Kevin's face.

"How about I get you some water brought in?" Marren offered.

"Don't open the door or I will blow my head off do you understand?" Kevin spit the words out.

"Yes, I do," Marren confirmed. "Don't do that. Talk to me Kevin, what can I do to get you to put the gun down?"

"Nothing." The line went dead.

All law enforcement involved was listening to the exchange. Marren's supervisor walked over and asked, "Go again?"

"Yes. Let me give him a minute," Marren answered. She could hear chatter on the coms talking about a breach.

She responded, "No breach. No breach. Stand down. We need those children out of that courtroom."

She recognized two of the voices as Martin and Thomas and heard Alec calling out position changes. Marren called Kevin's cell phone again, watching the camera to see him answer. This time Kevin said nothing, just listened.

"It's Agent Quinn. Take a look at your children, Kevin. I can see them on the courtroom camera." She watched Kevin's head turn slightly in the way of his children. "They look scared for their dad. You can't leave them alone in this world. They need their father. This hasn't gone too far, we can fix this. You and me. Let everyone else leave and we will fix this together. You don't want your children to see you take your life, it will destroy them." Marren stopped speaking, watching the monitor. Kevin was emotional, crying and fidgeting like a man barely holding himself together. "You are a good father, fighting for your children, don't do anything that will make them think different. Let them come out." Marren waited. The call was disconnected. It felt too long to wait and all of a sudden, they could hear Kevin's voice through the door yelling, "GET OUT. EVERYONE OUT."

Marren nodded to the agents manning the doors, "Open just one door so he knows we are not coming in."

Men, women and children hurried out the doors. Marren's ear buzzed with chatter from both the Mobile SWAT team and the FBI agents arguing about a move to breach.

"No breach. Do you hear me? No breach. I'm going to get him out alive. Do not breach. Stand down SWAT. Stand down," Marren fired into her headset.

Marren listened for directions from Alec to his team. What she heard was Martin arguing those directions.

Marren spoke into her headset, "Remove Operator Martin from the building."

"You don't fucking tell me…" Martin started.

Martin was cut off, "I do fucking tell you. I'm in charge. Remove yourself or I have an agent ready to remove you."

Marren watched the room from the camera angles, it was clear. She pushed the button on her phone to connect a call with Kevin.

"I did what you wanted," Kevin answered.

"Thank you. I want to come in so we can talk this through. Will you let me?"

"Why? Why do you want to come in?" Kevin asked.

Marren answered, "I don't want to talk on the phone. Face to face, it's better that way. We can get more solved. I'll keep my distance."

Kevin didn't answer for several moments. He finally responded, "Just you."

Marren nodded to the agent standing at the door, "Ok. Just me. We need a few rules. You cannot point your gun at me. If you make a move to point your gun in my direction, I will have to shoot you. Do you understand?"

"Yes. I'm not going to shoot you. I would never shoot you." Kevin was crying.

"I believe that. Kevin, I just want to make sure we don't have any misunderstandings. I want us both to be safe. Stay right where you are ok? No sudden moves. We are going to talk right where you stand."

"Ok."

Marren walked to the door, "I'm coming in. Do you see my hand in the doorway?"

"Yes."

Marren had picked up the monitor, watching him as she advanced to the door. Kevin was standing in the same place with the gun to his head. She put the monitor on the ground and drew her gun.

Marren spoke in the phone, "Kevin, I'm holding my gun. I'm not going to point it at you. We both have guns in our hands. We are not going to point them at each other, right?"

"No, I won't. I won't hurt you," Kevin confirmed.

She looked at the agent watching the monitor. He signaled that she could enter. Marren walked in the courtroom cautiously. She gave Kevin a nod.

"I'm going to end the phone call, you can hear me, right?"

Kevin put his phone in his pocket. "I can hear you."

"Good."

Marren tucked her phone in her pocket, taking a few steps towards the middle of the courtroom, which was a good distance from the defendant's table.

"How are my kids?" Kevin asked.

Marren didn't mince words, "Afraid for their dad. They want you to walk out of here. How are you? Do you want something to drink?" Marren offered.

"No. I just want my kids."

Marren nodded, "I understand."

"It's too late. I'll never have them again after what I've done."

Marren shook her head, "That's not true. You have not hurt anyone. You are still here to fight for them. It's never too late. We can get this cleared up. You have to put the gun down so I can help you."

"I'm not going to do that. I can't live without my children. I can't." Kevin closed his eyes, readying himself.

"Stop. Kevin, Stop. Look at me." Marren waited then said sternly, "Look at me, Kevin."

Kevin's eyes met hers.

"The only way you will never see your children again is if you pull that trigger. Nothing is so bad that it can't be fixed. You have choices to make. Leave your children without a father or fight for them."

"I tried to fight for them." Kevin's tears ran down his face.

"A different judge, a new job, new city, lots of options for you. This is not your only option. You haven't hurt anyone; the only person you've pointed the gun at is yourself. Let me help you." Marren's voice was calm and gentle. She took a few steps forward.

Kevin stood looking at her, "Why do you want to help me?"

"I don't want to see your children grow up without their dad. I watched them on the monitor. They love you. Don't do this. Something like this will stay with them and I know you don't want that."

"I'm going to be arrested, right?" Kevin looked at her.

Marren nodded, "Yes, but all the legal stuff can be worked out. You didn't hurt anyone. You haven't threatened anyone. Those are important factors. Let me help. I can walk you out. Cover the handcuffs so your children won't see them. You can get it all sorted out. The most important thing is you are alive to see your children again."

Kevin's free hand went to his face, fingers pushing his eyes. "I'm so fucked."

"No, no you're not. Take your finger off the trigger. I don't want you to make a mistake. Kevin, look at me." Marren waited. When Kevin looked at her, she continued, "Take your finger off the trigger. Let's walk out of here together. You have family, they will get you a lawyer. Nobody has been hurt. The court will go easy. Come with me."

The negotiations for Kevin's life went on for nearly an hour. Kevin agreed to remove his finger from the trigger but still held the gun to his head. He told Marren the story of his children's births. Kevin talked about their grades and school plays. She listened intently.

"You have wonderful children, that you love dearly. Don't leave them. Get things worked out so you can be part of their lives. Place the gun on the table."

"You'll hide the handcuffs? You will put me in the car?" Kevin wanted confirmation.

"Yes. My team is listening. I'll walk you out," Marren nodded.

Kevin lowered the gun from his head and placed it on the table.

"I need you to step away from the table towards me. Will you put your hands on your head for me? It's just us. I'm going to walk to you and put you in handcuffs." Marren stepped forward watching Kevin do exactly as she instructed. When she reached him she holstered her weapon. "Give me your left hand." Marren took his left hand, putting it in handcuffs, then took his right hand, securing it. "We are going to get a jacket to drape over the handcuffs. I need to check your pockets. My team is going to open the doors and come in. Nobody is going to touch you, ok?"

Kevin nodded and said, "Ok."

The courtroom doors opened with four agents stepping inside, weapons drawn but not pointed.

"He's secure." Marren commented, looking at the team. She took Kevin's arm, "Let's go. My partner is waiting with his jacket for you."

Marren could see Tim just beyond the door holding his jacket for her. Marren placed Kevin in the car, like she promised. She shut the door and stepped away. Alec stood waiting for her.

"You, good?" He looked at her with millions of eyes watching both of them. The local news teams, agents, SWAT, everyone was watching so Alec kept his distance.

"I'm good. I want Martin suspended." Marren was all business. "He could have cost people their lives today. I'm taking it to my superior and the chief."

"It's already done," Alec nodded.

"Thank you."

Marren soaked in the bathtub with soft music playing. She was on her second glass of wine and her third round of tears. The day had been rough. She was exhausted but it was too early to go to sleep. Alec had sent her a text message that he was tied up with paperwork and a meeting regarding the day's events. Marren's head rested on the edge of the tub with her eyes closed when Alec finally walked in.

Alec took a look at the bottle of wine on the bathroom floor missing a couple glasses. Marren's eyes were closed but he could tell by the rosy color around them that she had been crying.

He stripped out of his clothes. "Move forward baby." Alec got in behind Marren so her body would rest against him. He looked at her fingers, "You've been in here awhile."

"Yes."

Alec's hands washed over her, bringing water to her shoulders.

He spoke gently, "You did good work today. Good outcome. He was processed and sent to the hospital."

Marren nodded, "I thought he was going to do it." Her voice broke. "I watched him close his eyes and get ready to take the shot."

"He didn't do it. You talked him out of it," Alec said thoughtfully, kissing her temple.

Marren closed her eyes, leaning her head back on Alec. "There is too much sadness in the world. So many people doing things to each other or themselves. I'm tired of it."

Alec kissed her temple again, "Let's get you out of here. I'll feed you and we can talk cuddled up in bed."

"When we have a baby, I don't want to do this anymore." Marren's cheek rested on Alec's chest. His arms were wrapped around her with his lips kissing the top of her head frequently while they lay in bed.

Alec stroked her hair, "Why wait? You don't have to work. We can be comfortable without your income."

"There's no reason for me to stop working yet." Marren kissed his chest. "Plus I should finish the training I started with Mobile PD."

Alec flipped her on her back, "If you need a reason, I'll get you pregnant right now." He smiled, kissing her lips. "I want you to quit. I know that's not fair and that this has been your career but I don't want you working with SWAT. Let's get pregnant. Move up the wedding."

Marren kissed Alec, "We can't do that. I love what we have planned. I need time to decide what's next. Maybe teaching? You can't get me pregnant just because you want me to quit my job." Marren touched Alec's face.

"That's not the reason. We want to have a family. I'm just getting everything I want sooner rather than later. I love the baby making part." Alec moved his body between Marren's legs. "We get married, get pregnant and you choose a different career. That's what I want. Give me what I want." His voice was sweet while kissing down her body.

"Alec, I want that too. Just give it a little time. I need to do the right thing with the FBI in case I ever want to go back. I will start looking at teaching positions for the fall semester." She raked her fingers through Alec's hair.

"Promise? We get through the training and you take the summer off while we work on getting pregnant." Alec kissed the inside of her thigh, moving his lips towards her center.

Marren made a soft noise, "This isn't fair. Doing this to me while we…" Marren couldn't continue her sentence as she felt Alec's tongue taste her. "Alec."

"You told Alec about wanting to be a teacher. He is so happy," Addison said from the passenger seat with a smile on her face. "Are you?"

The women had spent Saturday afternoon enjoying lunch and wedding dress shopping.

Marren glanced at her, "I am happy. I'm ready for the next chapter. Marrying Alec, starting a family, everything I've wanted for so long." Marren giggled, "It's really happening."

Addison smiled, "It is, and you found your wedding dress. Your mom is going to light up when she sees you in it. My brother is going to be weak in the knees."

Marren's smile was beautiful, "I hope so."

"I know so," Addison smiled bright.

The police lights and siren surprised the women. Marren looked in her rearview mirror and Addison turned her head, looking behind her.

"Were you speeding?" Addison asked.

"No. Get your cell phone out," Marren told Addison.

Marren pulled over, retrieved her license, FBI badge, insurance and registration, rolled the window down, and put her hands on the steering wheel.

The officer approached, "Please step out of the car with your hands visible."

Marren spoke, "I'm FBI. Why are you pulling me over?"

"Do you have a weapon?"

"Yes, two. One in my purse and another under the seat," Marren answered.

"Step out of your vehicle, keep your hands visible," the officer instructed again.

Marren opened the car door. "Call Alec," she said to Addison.

Marren stepped out of the car, receiving instructions to put her hands on the car. The officer patted her down for a weapon.

The office stated, "This car has been reported stolen."

"My ID is in my hand."

She waved her hand slightly for the officer to take them.

The officer looked everything over, "I need to call it in. I'm going to cuff you while I do that."

Marren was furious, "That is not necessary. I'm FBI. My badge is in your hand. Allow my passenger to give you my registration so you can see the car is not stolen."

"I'll call your ID in. I'm going to cuff you while I do that."

The officer cuffed her, having her stand against her car. His partner stepped up while he walked to the car, checking her identification.

"Agent Quinn. Nice to see you. You look lovely." Operator Thomas looked at Marren with a sleazy smile.

Marren shook her head, "You could have cleared this up."

"Martin says hi," Thomas commented.

He looked back to see another police car pull up and the officer returning.

"Agent Quinn, I want to apologize. The vehicle description and tag were a mistake." The officer took her handcuffs off. "Again, I want to apologize, this was a mistake."

Marren rubbed her wrists, watching a lieutenant step forward, "Agent Quinn are you ok?"

Marren nodded, "Yes. Thank you."

The lieutenant told the officer and Thomas to return to their car. He walked to Marren's car, eyeing the two officers as they got in the squad car.

He looked back at Marren, "Alec called me. Are you sure you're ok?"

"I'm fine. I can go?"

"Of course. I'm going to follow you until you get to Daphne. Alec is on his way to Daphne, meeting me half way to escort you the rest of the way home."

Alec paced back and forth in the kitchen, "That's it you are done with this. That mother fucker is letting you know he can get to you. No more SWAT. I mean it." Alec looked at her, "I'm not kidding, you tell your supervisor that you're done."

Marren sat silent at the island sipping a beer.

"Are you seriously sitting there drinking a beer? Calm as a cucum-ber?" Alec's eyes were wild.

"You are upset enough for the both of us." Marren took another drink of her beer.

"What do you have to say?" Alec looked at her.

Marren stood, "Let's take a shower. I need to think about how to handle this."

"You are going to give notice," Alec directed.

"No, I'm not. Martin is not going to dictate my career. He's getting me back for the suspension. I'll handle it." Marren pulled her shirt over her head, walking towards the bedroom. She looked back, "Are you coming? I'll let you have me any way you want."

Alec was frustrated, "That's not going to work."

Marren reached behind her back unclasping her bra and removing the straps from her arms, "It's a shame I'll be lonely in the shower. I'll have to soap my body up all by myself."

Alec shook his head, following her to the bathroom.

CHAPTER 16

"A re you sure about this?" Tim asked Marren. "I can take lead today. Run the drill. It will be the same message."

Marren nodded, "I'm sure. If you run the drill, it won't be the same message."

Tim sighed, "Alec is going to be pissed. Should you give him a heads up?"

"He knows I'm demonstrating hand-to-hand combat today. Alec is not thrilled and will be on alert." Marren opened the doors to the gym.

Tim followed, "Ok, let's do this."

Tim addressed the SWAT operators while standing in the middle of the gym next to a parked car that they planned to use for the demonstration. The car was an Audi Q7, the same as Marren's car. Protective mats were placed at the side of the car. He explained the exercise would be to disarm and apprehend an auto theft suspect.

Marren stepped up, "Let's get started. Thomas, thank you for volunteering. Come on up."

Marren twirled two unloaded guns used for training. Thomas was shocked. He didn't volunteer but everyone was looking at him, waiting for him to step forward, so he did.

"Thomas, would you like to start as the suspect or officer?" Marren offered.

With a smirk on his face Thomas answered, "No difference."

Marren nodded, "Ok I'll be the officer. She handed him one of the guns, put that on you."

Marren addressed the group of men setting the scene. Thomas got in the car and Marren approached, asking him to get out. When Thomas stepped out of his car and reached for his gun, Marren apprehended him with force. She cuffed him, leaving him on the mat face down while she explained the maneuvers she demonstrated on Thomas.

"Let's go again." Marren uncuffed Thomas, holding the car door for him to get in. "This time Thomas will be unarmed and go for my gun."

Marren stepped to the car, instructing Thomas to get out with his hands visible. Thomas followed the direction but immediately tried to get the drop on her. Marren put him down in seconds. She cuffed him and again explained the different maneuvers she used to the group. Alec and Tim stepped forward, guarding the demonstration after listening to the comments that Martin was saying under his breath. It was clear that Marren was proving a point with how Thomas was getting worked over. Marren knelt down next to Thomas, removing the handcuffs.

She spoke quietly for only Thomas to hear, "You can tell Martin, I said hi."

The cuffs came off and she announced that she and Thomas would be switching positions. Marren got in the vehicle armed. Thomas made the announcement to step out of the vehicle with her hands visible. Marren stepped out of the car, put her hands on the hood like Thomas asked. When he stepped forward to complete a body search for her weapon, Marren had him on the ground with her gun to his head. Thomas had no time to reach for his gun before she had overpowered him.

Marren's voice boomed, "You're dead."

Marren looked up addressing the group. She explained what Thomas did wrong and that he would be dead because of his mistake.

Marren stood again, addressing the group, "I will be unarmed and going for his gun." She looked at Thomas, "Let's go again."

Thomas was sweating and pissed off. His voice was low, "I got your point."

Marren had no emotion on her face, "You sure. Or do you need to check with Martin?" Marren got in the car.

They ran through the routine again with Marren stepping out of the car. This time Thomas tried to take her down immediately. He was aggressive and out to hurt her. She was ready for him. Marren changed her tactics and not only took him down but took his gun from him, pointing it to the back of his head, her knee stuck in his back.

"You're dead."

Tim stepped forward turning to the group and explaining the new tactic and what Thomas did wrong. He had Alec step forward and showed the group what Thomas should have done different. Meanwhile Marren got up, stepping to the side of Thomas.

When Thomas stood his demeanor changed, "I apologize. You won't have any problems from me."

Marren nodded.

Marren was swaying to the music in the kitchen and chopping vegetables for a salad when Alec walked in from work.

Marren looked up with a smile, "Hi handsome. Dinner is almost ready. I made shrimp and fettuccine. I'm just finishing the salad. How was the rest of your day?"

Alec was proud but angry at the same time, "So kicking Thomas' ass today was how you decided to deal with Martin and getting pulled over?"

"I think I made my point. Thomas apologized after the ass whooping," Marren smirked. "It was a good demo and the group showed that they could unarm a suspect without weapons being fired. Today was a win. No excessive force and everyone did what they were supposed to do, including Martin."

Alec sighed, "Yes they did, but…"

Marren cut him off, "No more work talk. I made a delicious dinner. Take a look at the backyard; I'm so excited with the progress. It's going to be beautiful. Will you take me for a walk after we eat, hold my hand and say sweet things to me?"

Alec approached her taking her face in his hands.

His lips lowered to hers, "You are so beautiful." He kissed her madly. "I'm going to change for dinner and that walk you want to go on."

After dinner they walked hand in hand downtown, stopping at Mr. Bean's for ice cream.

Alec took a couple of spoonfuls in his mouth before he said, "I want you to take a step back with the training. Let Tim take the lead. I know that is not how you normally operate but please do this."

Marren thought for a moment, "Alec, I'm not going to stop doing my job. Please stop asking me to. I'm going to make a career change soon but until then, it's business as usual. I want to leave the FBI doing exactly what I've been doing for the last eight years, excellent work."

Alec was frustrated. He knew what she wanted to do was reasonable but the men she was dealing with were not reasonable.

"I can't get a good read on these guys other than they think they are above the law. It's only a matter of time before IA has enough on them. I'm not sure what they are capable of and for some reason you are on their radar. At first I thought it was because you are a woman and in charge, now it's turning out to be something more. That stunt Martin pulled, calling in your vehicle as stolen, was bold. My concern is that your so-called training with Thomas today is going to get a response from Martin."

"And if so, I'll deal with it. Let him come for me, it gives IA what they need," Marren said with confidence.

"Are you crazy? No, absolutely not. What are you trying to prove? It's crystal clear your training is far superior, let that be enough and step away from this."

"I'm not trying to prove anything. I'm doing my job. Yes, I was more forceful than I needed to be with Thomas today, but damnit he had it coming. I was put in handcuffs, Alec. On the side of the road, patted down for a weapon and cuffed. You think I'm going to just shrug that off? Would you?" Marren lost her interest in the ice cream and tossed it in the trashcan. "I'll meet you at home." Marren walked away.

Alec sat on the edge of their bed waiting for Marren to walk out of the bathroom. His eyes roamed her body then met her eyes.

"If they hurt you, if anything happens to you, I don't want to think about what I would do to the bastards."

Marren walked to him naked, putting her fingers in his hair, "I won't be in their face. I'm going to do my job but when it comes to Martin and Thomas, I'll keep my distance."

Alec kissed across her breasts, wrapping his arms around her body, "Thank you."

He flipped her onto the bed so she was flat on her back. Standing in front of her he took his clothes off, watching her eyes roam his body. He smiled when she chewed at her bottom lip.

"See something you want?"

Marren's eyes found his, "All of you."

"Good because you have all of me." He leaned over her, kissing her mouth so intensely it was more like he was making love to her mouth. His hand took hers, moving them above her head, "Keep your hands right here."

Alec stood at the edge of the bed between her legs, bracing himself with one arm resting on the bed so he was hovering over Marren. His eyes watched his fingers touch her cheek and lips, then roam down to her breasts. He teased her nipples, pinching and twirling his fingers until they were tight and hard. He leaned over, giving each a nibble and hollowing his cheeks suckling, them inside his mouth. He heard Marren's soft moan and looked up at her.

He bounced his eyebrows, "You come when I say."

His fingers moved between her legs, touching her in just the perfect spot. He stroked from her opening back to the spot that made her whimper, feeling her warm and wet. "Spread your legs for me."

Marren opened up more for him to do what he wanted. His fingers were gentle, flicking and swirling around, making her chase them with her hips. He watched her try to get more contact by lifting her hips up to meet his hand.

Alec continued with his plan, "I'm going to make you so crazy you beg to come." Alec's eyes burned with lust. He watched Marren clasp his forearm with one of her hands. "Do as you're told." His voice was gentle but commanding. Marren's hand moved back above her head. His fingers slid inside her, arching to find the place that tickled her from within. He wiggled his fingers within her walls before setting a pace an in and out motion.

"Oh God." Marren's back arched off the bed.

Alec watched her body surrender to every touch, every plunge and pull. His mouth sank to her breast with his lips and teeth taking her nipple in forcefully. Marren cried out in pleasure from the sensation, not only between her legs but from her breast. Alec slowed his fingers and backed off her breast. His kisses were felt down her stomach. He took her knees in his hands pushing them up and out opening her wide, his mouth didn't waste any time suckling her in. His tongue plunged inside her, causing a tremble in her legs. Alec knew she was close; just a few strokes of anything he did would send her over. His mouth kissed up her thigh to her knee. "You are so beautiful, baby. I love the way you taste. I'm going to slide my cock in, sound good?"

"Yes, yes."

Marren's hands moved, brushing her hair from her face and back to the place he left them above her head. Alec teased Marren's center with the tip, rubbing her, dipping in slightly and rubbing her on the outside again.

"You are so wet." Alec slid half way in, pulling back out to watch Marren's hips lift to take him.

He moved in and out a few quick times, pulling away to suck on her with his mouth.

Marren's body shivered, "Please, Alec."

Alec slid his fingers inside her while his teeth nibbled at her; his fingers were clenched before he removed them, only to plunge his tongue inside.

"I want you inside me." Marren's whimper was sexy.

Alec's tongue took a long taste, flicking and teasing before his mouth moved up her stomach to her breast. When his lips sucked her nipple in, he thrust inside Marren hard and deep, feeling her again on the edge. Marren wrapped her legs around his thighs, keeping him in place.

Alec only circled his hips, not taking her yet. He lifted to look at her face, "Feel good?"

She nodded with wild eyes, "Move, baby I want you to move."

Alec slid in and out gently as his mouth kissed her neck and his hand cupped her breast.

"You feel so good." Alec moved away, his face diving between her legs.

His lips and teeth tugged at her, sucked and prodded until she could barely breathe.

"Please Alec, make me come. I need to come. I can't take it, I can't..." Her voice was silenced when Alec's cock thrust inside. He pounded into her until she cried out his name with heavy breathing. Marren's entire body trembled from the climax. She pulsed around him in waves to Alec's slowing pace.

He flipped her on her stomach, lifted her hips and sank back in, "Now this way. I want you to come again right now." Alec slammed into her feeling her clench him tight. His hand spanked her ass. The bedding muffled Marren's screams of pleasure. "That's right, you come when I say. It's better that way." Alec pulled her hips, thrusting in hard and deep until he released in a wild groan. He held inside her with his sweaty face collapsing on her back. Moments later, he slid out and his body fell next to her with his arm pulling her to him. "I love you."

Marren managed to return the sentiment before she completely surrendered somewhere between being relaxed and incoherent.

CHAPTER 17

A lec sat on a stool at the kitchen island waiting for Marren. He looked at his watch, "Baby, we are going to be late to our own party. You look gorgeous."

Marren walked out of the bedroom, "How would you know that? I didn't have any clothes on when you left the bedroom."

"Exactly." Alec stood walking to her, "You are breathtaking. Let's get this done so I can get you back here."

Marren giggled, "Already undressing me, we haven't even left."

"I can't help it." Alec's hand took the side of Marren's face lifting it for a steamy kiss.

"Do you like this outfit?" Marren asked.

She wore a strapless, black, floral patterned corset, sexy but not too revealing, and white dress pants that fit perfectly. Her sandals were black and open toe.

"You look amazing." Alec kissed her temple. His hand stroked her thick dark hair that was soft with a slight wave under his fingers. "Everything about you looks beautiful and perfect."

"You look handsome. I love you dressed up. Actually, I love you in anything you wear or don't wear." Alec wore a white button down collared shirt and tan dress pants. Marren ran her hands up his chest, "You are so sexy." Marren lifted her face to his, taking another kiss.

The Pillars was decorated with candles and flowers, soft music played, and a member of the serving staff presented a tray of champagne when guests arrived.

Marren smiled wide, "Your sister and Max went all out for us."

Alec smiled with a nod, "Yes they did."

His hand held Marren's lower back, walking into the foyer of the restaurant. They took a glass of champagne and were immediately bombarded with hugs and congratulations from family and friends. Marren was surprised and ecstatic to see all of Alec's friends from DC, her parents, and their friend's parents. Her brothers would be in attendance for the wedding but couldn't get leave for the engagement dinner.

"You look beautiful, my girl." Marren's dad kissed his daughter's cheek. "Alec, you clean up nice." The colonel gave his soon to be son-in-law a pat on the shoulder and handshake.

"Thank you, sir. I see Mrs. Quinn had some influence on your clothes as well." Alec smiled.

"Alec, start calling me mom," Mrs. Quinn said, stepping forward and hugging Alec. She turned to Marren, "You are always lovely, sweetheart."

"Thanks, Mom. You look very pretty. Have you been introduced to most everyone?"

Both of Marren's parents nodded. "Anyone we haven't met, we can introduce ourselves. Enjoy your night. You have lots of people to say hello to." The colonel smiled and nodded.

The night progressed with toasts and stories through an amazing dinner. After dessert everyone stayed to mingle and enjoy additional cocktails. The men stood at the bar while the women talked wedding dresses at the table.

"Marren told her mother she is looking for a teaching position for the fall. I have to say I'm thrilled. I want grandchildren and I want my daughter working a job that doesn't have anything to do with your SWAT team," The colonel said to Alec.

"I want the same thing, sir. Your daughter is stubborn with a mind of her own." Alec looked at Marren, who smiled, meeting his gaze. "I wouldn't have it any other way but convincing her to leave the FBI now is impossible. I was hoping she would take the summer off, enjoy our home, just relax," Alec responded.

"I have no idea where she gets that stubborn streak," the colonel laughed.

Alec lifted an eyebrow, "No idea?"

"This was a perfect night, all our friends and family just the way we wanted it. I can't believe the DC crew flew in for dinner." Marren smiled, holding Alec's hand as they walked to the car.

Alec raised her hand, planting a kiss, "Of course they did. Any excuse to hug you and try to lure you away," Alec smirked.

Marren looked at him, "Not a chance. I'm so in love with you. I'm happy, truly happy, with you. We are going to have a wonderful life Mr. Jacobs," Marren smiled.

"Do you realize I get to call you Mrs. Jacobs in just a couple months? I can't wait until July. You will officially be mine."

The wedding was set for the first Saturday in July. Alec opened the car door for Marren. She smiled and turned to him.

"I am officially yours no matter the vows. I couldn't be more yours other than the paperwork." Marren put her arms around his shoulders.

Alec kissed her with the intention of getting her naked. His arms wrapped around her waist, but his hand wandered to her butt cheek, cupping it and pulling her to him.

"We need to go so I can get inside you. I love you, baby."

"I love you." Marren hugged him as her lips caressed his neck.

Martin spotted his lieutenant standing outside of The Pillars, an expensive, trendy restaurant, talking to a group of guys that looked like they were in the same line of work. He turned his car around and parked across the street to watch whom exactly the lieutenant hung around in his time off. Martin found Alec to be a mystery, never sharing personal information other than job and military experience. Martin watched Marren walk out of the restaurant with several women. She took Alec's hand, walked to his car together and shared an embrace that wasn't the first and beyond friendly.

Martin shook his head saying out loud, "I'll be damned, he's fucking the special agent."

CHAPTER 18

Training on Wednesday afternoon in mid-March was status quo. The team was scheduled a full day of training, first firearm and then hand-to-hand combat. Marren had done what she said, she limited her interaction with Martin, Thomas and the other men Martin seemed to influence. Tim had taken an active role in being a go between.

Alec was running through drills when his phone vibrated and he pulled it from his pocket to read the text message.

Marren: I can't concentrate with your shirt off. All I can think about is you above me making me cry your name.

Alec gave a half grin as he looked at the phone, taking a drink from his water bottle. He dropped the grin, looking up to see Marren talking to a SWAT member. She glanced at him briefly without any tell on her face. Alec's face was serious not to give anyone the impression he was enjoying the message exchange.

Alec: You're naughty and I'm going to spank you when I get home. Be naked waiting for me.

Marren felt the vibration in her pocket, "Excuse me," she said to the operator she was speaking to.

She pulled the phone out, reading the message. Marren gave a nod, feeling Alec's eyes on her but didn't look up. She placed the phone back in her pocket.

"Agent Quinn, an apple for the teacher." Martin approached Marren, offering a perfect shiny red apple. His gesture was intentionally offered in front of everyone.

Marren smirked with surprise and the acknowledgment that something was up, "Thanks, Martin."

Marren took the apple out of his hand.

"I know my impression of an asshole has gone a little far, so I want to call a truce. I apologize and I hope you will accept."

"No problem." Marren's head shot up slightly in a reverse nod to acknowledge the apology. Even though she knew Martin was full of shit, she played along with his gesture.

Martin went on, "As a matter of fact, a couple of the guys and I are getting together for some beers at the Bicycle Shop, it's a pub on Dauphin Street. If you're free, come hang out with us, I'll buy. Who knows, maybe we'll be friends."

Marren offered a weak smile, "Thank you for the invitation but it's against the rules to socialize with the team I'm training. You guys have a good night. Thank you for the apple."

Marren stepped away to answer a question Tim was waiting to ask her.

Tim looked at her, "I don't need anything. Just wanted to play interference. You know that's a poisoned apple right?"

Marren lifted a brow, "Ya, think? What's he up to? There's a play here."

"We'll find out soon enough. Alec doesn't look happy," Tim said with a nod, looking at Alec.

Alec stepped in the doorway of their bedroom, his face lit up with a grin and his eyes were full of desire.

"What are you reading?" he asked.

Marren was naked lying on her side in the middle of their bed, flipping through a magazine.

"Modern Bride," she answered with a grin, enjoying the look on Alec's face.

Marren's mind was already thinking of the weekend and how hectic it would be with Addison's baby shower on Sunday. Addie had insisted that they all meet for a pre-baby shower celebration including the guys on Saturday night at Bone and Barrel. One of the bands that the group enjoyed was playing. Marren knew it was a much-needed night out for everyone, she could feel the tension and toll everyone's work schedule was taking on them. Especially Alec, but his tension was aimed more towards her work choice. The week had been particularly difficult with Martin changing his game up from disrespectful to flirtatious and attentive. Martin had turned in to an ass kissing fool. He volunteered for every demonstration, followed Marren around, opening doors and doing any heavy lifting. He managed to flirt, compliment, and invite her to lunch in front of Alec. Martin even went so far as to ask Alec for advice on bridging the gap from friendship to dating.

"That would mean you would have to be a friend first. According to your stories you barely get a name before the girl is in your bed," Alec laughed with sarcasm, trying to deflect his annoyance.

Martin chuckled, "I'm an old dog trying to learn some new tricks. I think Agent Quinn is beginning to think of me as a friend instead of a foe. This training won't last forever so I figure put in some time as a friend now before I make my move."

"Good luck," Alec smirked, fastening his belt.

He sat down to put on his shoes. The team was changing out of their workout gear into street clothes at the end of their shift.

"I don't need luck with my good looks," Martin strutted.

Another operator on the team piped up, "That sweet thing is out of your league, too smart for you. Stop pumping iron and read a book."

The locker room was filled with laughter and additional comments teasing Martin.

Martin held both arms wide, "What's a guy gotta do? I'm trying to change my ways, get in her good graces. I think I'm wearing her down. Y'all are going to be jealous when that sweet thing is on my arm."

Alec was finished getting ready, "Have a good weekend fellas."

CHAPTER 19

Marren walked in the house after attending Addison's baby shower. It was a perfect mid-May day and besides Alec being grumpy, the shower went off without a hitch. Addison felt completely loved and her bundle of joy celebrated. It was obvious to everyone at the shower that Alec was upset with Marren by the scowl on his face. Alec and Max arrived at the end of the shower to load the gifts to take home.

Hearing the water running, she found Alec in the backyard watering the new landscaping. She walked out the sliding doors, handing him a glass of iced tea.

"Say your peace so you'll stop giving me the evil eye."

"I don't think you want me to say my peace."

Marren shook her head, "No, I would much rather you brood and give me the cold shoulder. That's so much fun." She sat down at the new patio table. "Come on, let's talk."

Alec released the nozzle on the hose to stop spraying water. He wound the hose and walked over to the table.

He stood at the table and leaned towards her, bracing his hands on the table, "You know exactly how I feel. Type up a resignation letter, give the FBI notice and end this."

He turned, walking in the house and slamming the French door. Marren's anger moved through her like electricity. She shot out of the chair, following Alec in.

"You don't dictate to me! I've been with the FBI for nine years. I will make a change when the time is right. Don't talk to me like you are running the show. We are in this life together. I'm interviewing for a teaching position."

"You will do what I say! I'm not going to have you in harm's way. I've had enough." Alec pointed at Marren, "What do you have to prove? You've accomplished more in your career than most. You don't need to work. Take a much deserved break. Walk away before you are hurt." Alec hesitated, "Before you hurt our relationship. Put me fucking first for once!"

His voice boomed and he watched her expression change from anger to hurt. Alec thought he may have gone too far but he was livid. Training was nearing the end and it came from the commissioner on Friday that Marren and Tim would stay on with SWAT working cases and be scheduled in the team's weekly rotation. They were taking on a bigger role with IA building a case against Martin and possibly additional officers who were suspected of extortion and bribery with a local drug gang.

Marren's eyes filled with tears. Her voice was low and upset, "For once? That's how you feel? I don't put you first?" Tears ran down her cheeks. "You want me to walk away from the only consistent thing I've known since college; the thing that I relied on when my heart was broken, how I met friends when I moved here. And why should I be forced out because of some asshole?" Marren wiped her tears.

Alec knew he wasn't being fair, but the threat was real, "Be my wife. Let's get pregnant. Let that be enough until a teaching job comes along."

Marren's tears continued, "Because you would do that for me? You would give up your career? I think you proved you wouldn't sacrifice what you worked for to be with me until the right thing came along."

Alec's temper got the best of him. Through clenched teeth he hissed, "You will quit. If you want a life with me, you will leave the FBI immediately."

Alec snatched his keys off the table by the front door. He walked out, slamming the door behind him.

Marren stood at the kitchen counter chopping vegetables for a salad when Alec returned. He had been gone several hours; it was nearly 8'oclock.

When he didn't say anything, just walked to their bedroom, she followed him. "Did you eat dinner?" She watched him pack his gym bag but when she realized he was packing more than workout clothes, she swallowed hard. "Where are you going?"

"I ate at the brewery. I'm going to the other house. I think we need to think about things. I need a breather. We've been fighting about the same thing on and off for a month and we need a break from it."

Marren walked out of the bedroom. She took her glass of wine to the back patio so she didn't have to watch him leave.

"Alec?" Addison called, walking in Alec's house. His SUV was parked in the driveway.

"Kitchen," Alec answered.

Addison walked to the edge of the kitchen, carrying a tote of decorations from the baby shower.

"Marren gave me the key last week. She said it was ok for me to store decorations for y'all's bridal shower over here."

Alec nodded, standing at the stove and folding over an omelet.

"What are you doing?" Addison asked

Alec gave her a sideways glance, "This would be cooking." He chuckled knowing his comment was smartass. His sister was at best a lousy cook.

"Funny." She rolled her eyes. "Why are you cooking here? Where's Marren?"

Alec shrugged, "I'm hungry so I'm cooking."

Addison put her hands on her hips, "I love these worthwhile conversations. You're in a mood. What did you do? She boot you out of the house tonight?"

Alec shook his head, "No." He hesitated, "I needed a breather so I came over here last night."

Addison moved to a barstool at the kitchen island. "You left? Come on Alec, that's not how you handle a disagreement. You don't leave your house, argue it out."

"I'm tired of arguing. Marren either puts in her notice with the FBI or I might be living here permanently." Alec took the omelet off the stove, looking at it. Saying what he just said, his appetite was lost. He placed the plate on the counter with the perfect omelet looking back at him, "Hungry?"

Addison shook her head no, "You don't mean that. Please tell me you didn't say that to her."

When Alec looked at his sister it was obvious that was exactly what he said.

"How did Marren react?" Addison asked with concern.

"She didn't say anything. Left me alone to pack my overnight bag."

"How was work today?" Addison inquired.

"Tim said she was called to the courthouse so I didn't see her. And before you ask, I haven't talked to her. She hasn't reached out to me either." Alec stepped to the refrigerator, opening it for a beer.

"I thought you were hungry?" One of Addison's eyebrows lifted.

"You managed to ruin my dinner with your chatting."

"You ruined your own dinner because you left your fiancé." Addison hopped off the stool, smoothing her shirt over her baby bump. "If Max would have given me an ultimatum like that, we would have had a serious problem. You don't tell someone to give up what they worked for. Alec, you didn't give up your job in DC when you knew it was ruining what you had with Marren, but you expect her to do that."

"I wasn't in danger."

"You were in danger every day. She trusted you to keep yourself safe. She deserves that same trust." Addison picked her car keys up off the counter. "I hope you know what you're doing because I remember how miserable you were without Marren." She walked to the door, "See you later."

Marren, feeling unnerved, decided to reach out for reinforcements. She sent Tim a text message.

Marren: 911 need you. Dress in workout clothes for my self-defense class. Martin is here.

Thirty minutes later, Tim walked in, giving Marren a friendly wave, "Sorry, I'm late."

"No problem." Marren's smile was that of relief.

She went through the warm up exercises like she did every week, recapping the previous week's lesson. When Martin volunteered for a demonstration, Marren didn't miss a beat, bringing him up with Tim to demonstrate the self-defense maneuver that was simple compared to the training the two men had mastered in their careers. She brought up a female volunteer as well, showing the demonstration between two women, then paired the four volunteers so that the threat and counter could be demonstrated with male and female examples.

When the class finished it was typical for Marren's students to hang back and talk to her while she packed up her gym bag. Tonight was no different with the exception that Martin was taking everything in. Tim played interference in the hopes that Martin would not catch any personal information about Marren.

"Hey Martin, catching a refresher course?" Tim chuckled, standing maybe two feet from the mass of muscle.

"Slow night. Just looking for some fun, figured Agent Quinn's class would be amusing. Quite a few cougars looking for a good time," Martin scoffed.

Tim nodded with a slight grin that hid his annoyance, "You know it's against policy for Agent Quinn to interact with you socially."

Martin rolled his eyes, "I haven't seen her all week. I'm missing her. I wondered if I scared her off. No harm in checking on her."

"You can see she's perfectly fine. No need to check, the FBI takes care of their own. Marren is working an investigation like I explained on Tuesday." Tim crossed his arms against his chest, "Look I'm not trying to be a dick here but back off. I don't want to get your LT involved."

Martin gave a nod, knowing he accomplished exactly what he set out to. "Think my LT would take issue with me participating in a little extra training on my own time? Or is it that I'm fucking with his girl?"

"Get the fuck out of here. I'll address your extra training with command. You don't fuck with my partner and think you're not fucking with me."

Martin raised his hands like he was surrendering, "No harm, no foul just giving IA something to do. I figured this would be more exciting than sitting outside my house. Tell Agent Quinn I'll see her soon."

"Kiss your career goodbye. You're harassing a federal agent." Tim's voice was steady like he just stated a forgone conclusion.

Martin's chest jerked in a laugh before he turned leaving the building.

Walking out of the rec center Marren looked at Tim, "I didn't ask you to call him."

Alec stood next to her car door, waiting for her. His car was parked next to hers with Tim's car parked on the other side.

"You need surveillance. It's been called in. Alec needed to know. Two agents will be at the house when you get there. We have a meeting at 7am with IA and all the head honchos." Tim walked to her car, ready to turn her over to Alec. He placed his hand on her shoulder, "You ok?"

Marren gave a quick lift of her head, "I'm good. Thank you."

"That's what we do. We are partners and friends. See you in the morning." Tim looked at Alec, giving him a head nod as an acknowledgment and stepped away to his car.

Alec opened Marren's car door without saying anything. He felt the anger rolling off her in heavy pushes through the air. She slammed her body in the car seat and pulled the door closed.

"I have agents outside, no need to stay. You can go home." Marren walked in the door tossing her keys on the kitchen counter.

"You are my home."

Alec followed her into the bedroom where she was opening the safe. She took out her firearm and placed it on the top of the dresser. Marren opened dresser drawers, getting a clean tank top and panties.

She picked up the gun and her clothing, "I'm taking a shower and going to bed. You're not welcome in here."

Alec's eyes narrowed, "I'm staying. On the couch."

He opened his dresser taking out a pair of workout pants.

"That's not necessary. I have plenty of protection."

Alec turned to her, crossing his arms over his chest, "I'm not leaving. Get on board."

Marren hissed, "You left me! You walked out on me! I don't want you here!"

Alec moved so fast she was in his arms with his hand holding the side of her face, positioning her to look at him.

"I needed to cool down. Try to see it from your side. I love you, more than anything. If anyone hurts a hair on your head... I will kill him, do you get that? He's after you like it's some game. I can't think straight knowing you could be hurt. I don't know how to stand by and allow you to put yourself in danger."

Marren lifted on her toes, wrapping her arms around Alec's shoulders.

Her face nuzzled in his neck, her voice in a whisper, "You can't leave me. I need you, I can't be without you."

Alec felt his neck dampen with Marren's tears.

His voice immediately dropped in volume, "I don't know how to live without you. I'm never leaving you." His hand took her face, "I can't lose you. Do you understand what I mean? Martin is a dirty cop. He wouldn't hesitate to take your life if you are what is standing between him and his goal. You can't do that to me. Martin knows you're getting close. He feels the pressure, or he would never have tried to scare you tonight. That's what he's doing. He knows about us. He told Tim tonight that he's fucking with my girl. That's a warning. Let me take care of him. Please, Marren."

"Ok." Marren surrendered. Jeopardizing her life or life with Alec wasn't worth working with IA.

For the next two weeks Marren was needed in court for testimony regarding training and had a three-day orientation for new recruits. That left Tim and Alec to work together with IA investigating a money trail that they hoped would lead to Martin and two other officers, neither of which were on SWAT. Luck had it that they caught an important break. A routine traffic stop put a gang member in custody that was happy to give information on a shipment of drugs coming into Mobile Bay via boat from New Orleans. The gang member gave the information for a deal with less jail time.

Marren walked to the doorframe of Alec's office, giving it a knock. He looked up from his desk, giving her a smile.

She smiled back, "Bad time?"

"No come in, shut the door."

When the door was closed, he stood, coming around the desk to lean against it. His hand ran down Marren's forearm quickly. That's all the contact he could chance with a window that looked out to a busy hallway.

"How did it go?" Alec asked.

"Really good. I should know by the end of the week. The school board was impressed with my credentials. I hope I'm what they're looking for. They brought one other candidate back for a second interview. She has eighth grade teaching experience where I have no classroom experience with children."

Alec smiled, "I have a good feeling. They would be fools not to hire you. You are over qualified to teach tenth grade so they know this is something your heart is calling you to do. The way you light up, they know you're going to give it your all. The classroom experience won't outweigh what you have to offer." He winked at her. "You know I want to kiss the hell out of you right now."

Marren gave him a smile that showed up in her eyes, "I would enjoy you giving me one of your famous kisses."

"Famous, huh? How so?"

She giggled, "It's like a kiss from a movie or romance novel. I feel it in my toes. Your kisses set me on fire. Don't pretend like you don't know that."

Alec chuckled, "Your mouth does the same thing to me. How about a nice relaxing bath tonight and some kissing that leads to…" Alec bounced his eyebrows without finishing the sentence.

"You have a date." Marren's smile lit her face. "How are things here? Tim told me about the lead. Any news?"

"Waiting on Martin's next move. He knows we're watching him so he's played by the book the last two weeks but he's going to want a payment from the deal that's about to go down."

"Are the drugs in port?" Marren asked.

"Yes. They came in last night. No activity as of yet. I have Martin on my schedule the rest of the week. If he's going to do something on duty it will be during the day. Anything after hours, IA and the FBI have him."

"What about who he is working with?"

Alec blew out a breath in frustration, "They have suspects but no hard evidence."

Marren nodded, saying out loud what she was thinking, "I'm surprised Thomas isn't in on it. Martin has a lot of influence with him."

"He might be. If he is, I think he's a lap dog, just doing Martin's bidding. Thomas is not doing any real decision making. IA has him picking up a couple payments from a bar. Looks like he popped them for underage serving and Thomas made them a deal not to bust them in lieu of payment. We haven't moved on him trying to keep things quiet waiting on Martin." Alec changed the subject, "How are the new recruits?"

"Eager. I have their paperwork to finish up tomorrow morning then I'll be back here to work with your in-house firearms instructor. We are going to create a new course plan for your recruits and another for seasoned officers. If all goes well, I'll turn in my notice on Friday. My last day of work will be a week before our wedding."

"That's forty-five days. What happened to the standard two-weeks?" Alec asked.

Marren shook her head with a smirk, "I told you, I'm giving them plenty of time to replace me. If they don't need me, I'll take my vacation days and leave early."

"You know they are going to take you up on the time. They'll work your ass off until you go."

Marren shrugged, "I need to help transition someone in. Are you giving me a hard time?" She smiled, "This was a fair negotiation, we are both getting what we want."

Alec put his hands up, "You're right. Thank you for staying clear of this investigation. Knowing you are not in the equation and safe, I'm breathing easier. Plus, your dad is off my ass."

Marren laughed, "Both of you are a pain in my ass. What time will you be home?"

"I'm going to wrap up around six. I should be home by seven or seven thirty. Want sushi?" Alec asked.

"Sounds good. I'm going to do some shopping. I'll meet you at Master Joe's at 7:30." She smiled, "I love you."

"Love you. Be careful."

"Always."

CHAPTER 20

"Hey Baby, It's 7:30pm, I'm at Master Joe's. I got a table, just need my girl." Alec left a voicemail for Marren. He looked at the waiter, "I'll take a beer, Sapporo."

At 8pm Alec dialed Marren again.

"Hey LT, I lost track of time. Sorry you've been waiting on Marren to call and cancel your dinner plans."

Hearing Martin's voice on Marren's phone, Alec stood, immediately tossing a $20 bill on the table and walking to the exit.

"What the fuck are you doing Martin? Put Marren on the phone."

Martin chuckled, "You don't call the shots LT. You take your instructions from me. That job you are sitting pretty in should have been mine. Ever since you got here, you've been a thorn, and your girl... she's an awfully pretty thorn but just the same. Here's what we are going to do. You are going to move the drugs, collect my money and Marren and I will meet you for dinner. Better hurry, we're both hungry."

"Like hell I am. You are fucking with the wrong guy and my girl is a federal agent, you are so fucked. You won't be able to run fast enough, everyone will be after you."

Martin laughed, "You got it wrong. You will do exactly what I want or I'm going to introduce your girl to some of my friends. They don't like feds but pussy, they like that. Give us a call back when you've made the arrangements. And Alec, don't get creative, Marren's counting on you." The phone went silent.

Alec was in his car driving to Mobile by the time Martin hung up. He dialed Tim.

"Tim, tell me you're tracking Marren's phone. Martin has her."

"Let me call you back." Tim hung up.

Alec waited less than two minutes for Tim to ring back.

"Last ping was the precinct at 5pm. The app must have been re-moved."

"Fuck!"

Alec's head was spinning. He filled Tim in on what Martin requested during the call.

"No way you're going to be able to move that boat or get the drugs off the boat without the feds being involved. You are walking into a set up. Even if you could deliver the drugs, that group will kill you when you deliver, no way are you getting a payment for Martin. He's setting you up to look like the one on the take. You can't go this alone. Let us help."

"How is he going to explain Marren? He took her. He can't let her go and say it didn't happen. What's his end game? He's caught."

"Did you talk to her? Hear her in the background? What if he doesn't have her? Could he have lifted her phone? Maybe get you to deliver, then he never had Marren and you look guilty?"

Alec ran his hand over his face, "He has her. She didn't show up for dinner. Where the fuck is IA and the feds and how are we not getting intel on where he is and that he is with Marren?"

"IA is at his door now. His phone shows he's in his house. Car in the garage. He won't be there if he has Marren. Head to the marina, I'll meet you there. Alec, we'll find her."

Alec heard Tim's radio fill with chatter before he hung up. "What are they saying?"

"Martin's not there. His car and phone are at the house. We need to play this cool. Let me call you with a game plan."

"I'm moving the boat. Make sure your guys don't pick me up. Martin could be in Marren's car. I need the feds looking for her car. I don't know who is working with Martin so I can't call it in with the department." Alec disconnected the call.

Tim was waiting for Alec at the boat launch, "Let's do this."

Alec shook his head, "You can't come with me."

"You need someone watching your back."

"I'm moving the boat and calling Martin. Find them before I have to give him the location." Alec got on the boat while Tim untied the dock lines. "I'll call you."

Alec moved the boat to Dog River Marina. When he arrived at the marina, he was met by an agent that looked similar in build.

"Take my car, I'm taking point here. Dial me in to all calls to Martin. Here is a phone with the surveillance of this boat, it will be like you are here," the agent directed.

Alec punched Marren's number, with Martin picking up immediately. He didn't wait for Martin to speak.

Alec hissed, "I've got the boat. Bring Marren to me."

"That's not the directions I gave you. You'll need to meet with my friends and get my money."

"Your friends want their drugs. I'll let them know you're what's standing in their way. I'll head to The Pillars, you and Marren join me for dinner and I'll give you the location of the boat to share with your friends." Alec hung up, quickly dialing Tim. "Did you get a location?"

"We've been able to get the tower her phone is using but not the specific location. Her phone is in the Fairhope area. We are looking for her car." Tim knew that wasn't what Alec wanted to hear.

"He's calling back." Alec switched the phone over.

"I told you not to get creative, where is the boat? You will need to meet my friends in order to get your girl. That's if you want to see her happy and healthy."

"Martin, your friends don't give a shit about me or Marren. They will give a shit about you exposing them and you instructing me to take their drugs. I have one of their associates in custody. I'm sure he knows who to reach out to. Stop fucking around and put Marren on the phone. I want to hear her voice."

"Fuck you." Martin's voice boomed.

"You are the one that's fucked. Without the drugs, your friends are going to come looking for you. Everyone will be hunting you down. End this now, give me Marren and I'll tell you where the boat is." Alec heard a smack and a muffled whimper. "I'll kill you, Martin. You hurt her and I will kill you."

Martin laughed, "You keep thinking you're in charge, that's what's getting her hurt. Where is the boat?"

Alec looked at his phone when Tim's text message came through.

Tim: Your house.

Alec was already heading in the direction of Fairhope when he told Martin, "Dog River. Send your friends to Dog River. I'll meet them there."

"Good boy. I'll call you when they're ready to make the trade."

Alec drove for forty minutes, parking down the street from his house and finding Tim waiting in his car along with six additional agents spread out through the neighborhood. They had come up with a plan for Alec to be at the marina using an agent, when in reality they were going to surprise Martin at the house.

"As soon as we get the green light to make the exchange at the marina, we will put this plan in motion." Tim showed Alec the camera of the agent waiting at the boat.

Alec picked up the phone, dialing Martin, "What's the hold up? How much money should I be expecting?"

"My guys are almost there. 50k. You'll bring it to me, your girl's not very hungry so we are going to skip dinner. I'll give you a location to meet us after you have what I want."

Alec took a deep breath, "I want to talk to her."

"Yeah well, I'm not taking off the duct tape. I can smack her around a little so she moans for you. Want that? Just do what the fuck I tell you to. You are in no place to demand anything." Martin paused briefly and continued, "My guys are pulling up. Flash the console light so they know where you are."

Alec watched the video and the light flick on and off.

"Done," he announced. Watching three men approach carrying duffel bags, Alec wanted Martin to think he was at the meet, "Want to talk to your friends?"

"No wise ass, no need. Take the duffel with my money and their car."

Alec watched the agent receive the duffel and keys.

"Now what?"

"Head towards the bay way. I'll give you more specifics after I con-firm the drugs are safe with their owner." The line went dead.

Alec looked at Tim, "Do we have eyes in the house yet? It's time to move, we have about forty minutes max."

Tim's radio chirped with static then a hushed voice.

"He has the house ready to burn. The accelerant is going to limit what we can do, no firearms, no spark. Two heat signatures, one mov-ing, one stationary in the center of the house. Call him and see what his next move is."

Alec dialed Martin, "Well? Where am I going? I'm on the bay way."

"Stop at Felix's Fish Camp and wait for instructions." The line went dead.

The FBI agent pulled in Felix's parking lot where two black un-marked police cars pulled up on either side of the car he was driving. Martin's partners were surprised to see Alec was not in the driver's seat. Federal agents swarmed the three vehicles and Martin's partners were apprehended.

Martin called Alec.

"Thanks for delivering my money. You and your girl can see each other in the afterlife. By now you've both realized who is actually in charge. That would be me."

Alec spoke from inside the house, "No Martin, that's where you're wrong."

Martin startled to see Alec standing inside the back door of his house, pulling out his gun and pointing it at him. Alec smirked, "I know you're not going to shoot me, you might set yourself on fire. Accelerant on your hands."

Defiant, Martin said, "I'll set the whole place up, nothing to lose."

Alec shook his head, "You want to die in a fire? You're too big of a pussy to burn. Put the gun down and let's see if you actually paid attention to any of the training. I've wanted to kick your ass for a long time." While Alec spoke, he moved forward keeping Martin's attention and giving Tim time to find Marren and get her out of the house.

Martin grinned, "You don't give a shit that your girl is going to go up in flames? You'll burn the whole house down around you to kick my ass?"

"You're done Martin. We have your partners, the drugs, the money, everyone wrapped up in a nice little bow. The only way you're leaving this house is in handcuffs or in a body bag, you decide."

Alec moved forward again, stopping about ten feet in front of Martin. Martin charged Alec with both of them tumbling to the floor, the gun falling away. They wrestled and Alec felt the sting and flush of blood soak his shirt.

Lurching back, he hissed, "Of course you fight dirty."

They both moved, sizing each other up, Martin jabbing at Alec with his knife, Alec connecting a couple blows to Martin's upper body. When the front door busted open, Alec seized the opportunity to collapse his large arm around Martin's neck, cutting off oxygen flow. Martin's arms dropped and the knife fell to the floor. The adrenaline and aggression consumed Alec who was on the verge of breaking Martin's neck.

"Alec! Alec!" Tim shouted, "I've got her. Let him go, give him to Agent Morris."

Martin was a rag doll in Alec's arms. Agent Morris moved quickly to remove Alec from Martin's neck.

"Lieutenant! I've got him."

Alec stepped back, collapsing to his knees.

"We need some help!" Tim called, watching Alec press his hand against his abdomen.

"Where is she? I need to see her. Is she conscious?" Alec raged.

Addison spoke gently as she waddled alongside Alec's gurney. She and Max arrived at the hospital as Alec was being pulled from the ambulance.

"She's ahead of us. Stop Alec, or they will sedate you. You can't move like that with that gash. Max is going to stay with you. I'm going with Marren."

Before Addison moved ahead of them to find Marren, Max said, "Slow down." He was concerned the stress of the situation would put Addison into labor. She was already five days beyond her due date.

"I'm ok. Take care of my brother."

Max found Addison standing in the hallway outside of Marren's room.

"Your brother was taken to a procedure room to close the cut. It's too deep for the ER. How's Marren?"

"She just came back from a CAT scan. She has a concussion, two fractured ribs, lots of bruising. He beat her up, tossed accelerant on her." Addison put her hand over her mouth to stop herself from weeping, "He was going to burn her."

Max pulled her in his arms, "She's going to be ok."

Addison nodded, tears coming steady, "They have someone examining her eyes for permanent damage, both are swollen shut and they had to flush the gasoline out of them."

"Your brother is losing his mind that he isn't with Marren. He wanted the doctor to wait on stitching him up. The nurse told him Marren was in X-ray and she would bring him to her room as soon as the last stitch was tied. The waiting room is a mad house with police and

FBI. All our friends are here. Did you get a hold of Marren's mom and dad?" Max gave Addison a rundown of what he knew.

Addison nodded, "They are on their way to the airport."

Max and Addison stood outside Marren's room in silence for nearly fifteen minutes before Alec was rolled down the hall and the ER doctor approached the door holding Marren's chart.

"Hey Doc, I'm Alec Jacob's, Marren's fiancé. How is she doing?"

"Nice to meet you Mr. Jacob's. Marren is doing well all things considered. I'm headed inside, the specialist should be about finished with the eye exam."

Alec's face looked panicked, "I don't know the extent of her injuries, I was receiving treatment. What is happening?"

The doctor explained Marren's injuries, adding that he had ordered a consult with an OB.

"OB?" Alec looked confused.

The doctor offered a slight smile, "It's early, that's why neither of you has asked, you didn't know. From the HCG levels, I'm estimating Marren's six weeks pregnant. We need to make sure the baby is ok. We have an ultrasound machine on the way. She took a few kicks to the chest and abdomen."

Alec swallowed hard, "How do we tell her she's pregnant and the baby might not be ok? I need to be the one that tells her about the baby."

The doctor nodded, "Let's not get ahead of ourselves. The blood work shows a healthy pregnancy; one test at a time."

The technician rolled the ultrasound machine down the hall towards Marren's room. The doctor excused himself to talk to the OB doctor that was following the technician.

Addison touched Alec's shoulder, "Alec, prepare yourself. Marren is very banged up. Both of her eyes are swollen shut and bruised. She's in pain."

"Ms. Quinn, I'm done. I don't see any issues with your vision. The bruising and swelling look bad but no permanent damage." The eye specialist patted Marren's hand.

"Thank you, Dr. Harmon." Marren's voice was weak. "Will you check on Alec for me?"

"I'm right here, baby." Alec rolled his wheel chair in the room and to Marren's side. He took her hand, pressing his lips to her fingers. "I love you so much. You're going to be ok. I'm right here."

"Are you ok? What happened to you?" Marren's face turned in the direction of his voice. Tears slid down her face from the corners of her swollen eyes.

Alec's fingers were gentle, moving her hair away from her face, "I'm ok. Everything is going to be ok." He looked at her beaten and bruised face. "I'm so sorry, baby. I should have walked you to your car."

Marren's hand reached for Alec's face, feeling the damp from tears, "It's not your fault. I didn't see him."

Alec's face turned, kissing the palm of her hand, "I was so scared. You can never leave me." Alec stop speaking, taking in the feeling of her hand on his face. "We have a surprise." Alec's hand moved, resting on Marren's lower stomach. "You're pregnant."

Marren's voice was shaky as she whimpered, "Is the baby ok?"

"The doctor wants to run an ultrasound, make sure you and the baby are ok."

The ultrasound tech moved in, prepping Marren's stomach and getting the machine ready for the OB doctor.

Alec held Marren's hand whispering to her, "I love you more than anything. You're going to be my wife soon."

The thumping sound coming through the speakers brought relief to both Marren and Alec.

"That's the baby's heartbeat. Everything looks good. We are going to monitor you closely and have you come back for another ultrasound in two weeks, or follow up with your OB in two weeks just to be on the safe side."

CHAPTER 21

“The backyard is perfect.” Marren smiled, resting her head on Alec’s chest.

Kissing the top of her head, Alec agreed. “Perfect. And this chaise lounge is going to get a ton of attention this summer.” They were both sprawled out, taking the day nice and slow. Alec looked down at Marren’s face, it had been three weeks since she was released from the hospital. “Your eyes are looking better every day. Baby is healthy. You’re in my arms. Perfect day.”

Marren’s hand moved gently over Alec’s stomach where his stitches were removed a few days prior, “Feeling better?”

“Much.”

“Mmm. I could go for a little love making,” Marren flirted.

Alec kissed the top of her head, “Your ribs and the baby. Maybe we wait a little longer?”

Marren smirked, “My ribs are feeling better and you can’t hurt the baby.” Marren’s eyes met his, “I need you, Alec. I need us to go back to our life. Put this behind us.”

Alec gave her a nod, getting up from the chaise lounge, “We are getting back to normal. I just want to give it a little more time for you to heal.”

"Alec, are the bruises... I mean, do you still want me? Find me sexy?" Marren sat up.

"What? Of course I want you. I just want to be careful, make sure you're 100%. You're beautiful and sexy. Come on Marren, I love you so much. We are getting married, having a baby, you are everything to me." Alec leaned over and kissed the top of her head. "Burgers from the brewery still good for dinner?"

"Sure."

Alec walked in the brewery, placing his and Marren's dinner order with the bartender. "How's business Maggie?"

"Steady. We had a good early dinner rush."

Alec tapped his hand on the bar, "Excellent. Seth in the back?"

"He was in the back helping the line last I heard."

Alec walked in the kitchen, "Hey Seth."

"Alec. How are you feeling? How's Marren doing?" Seth walked to the office with Alec.

"I'm doing pretty good. Not hitting the gym yet but feeling more like myself. Marren is much better. Trying to keep her from doing too much. How are things this week? Thank you so much for helping with the schedules." Alec picked up a stack of mail and paperwork to take home.

"Don't think twice about it. Anything I can do to help out, you know I will. Ophelia said Marren gave notice, accepted the teaching position. I'm so happy for her. I bet you feel relieved."

Alec agreed, "She's excited to be teaching in the fall. I'm nervous for her to leave the house." Alec ran his hand through his hair, "I feel guilty. I should have been there, walked her to her car. You know he beat her because I took his job, because I went after him, he could have killed her." He shook his head, "I made her back off and because of that she let her guard down. I don't want her to leave the house without me."

"Alec, my understanding is you saved her. If it weren't for you, she wouldn't have made it. You have to let everything else go. Get back to the good. You both need to get back into your life, your routine of normal. Locking her away isn't going to work."

"How many times has he called today?" Addison asked rocking her baby boy.

Marren served two grilled chicken salads for a late lunch. Sitting the dishes down at the table she said, "Every hour. It's been four weeks, his official first day back behind his desk. He was nervous to leave me this morning. I don't think I've been out of his sight more than a couple hours since it happened."

Addison pressed her lips together, "I don't blame him. He wants to take care of you, keep you safe. Alec will ease up, give him time. Start doing what you love, you know? What you enjoy, and let him see life like it was. He's too in his head about what he could have done different."

"It's more than that. He feels responsible for what Martin did." Marren took a bite of her salad, swallowing. "He needs to talk to me about it so he can put it behind him. So we can move forward together."

Addison offered an explanation, "Alec and I have never been great at talking about the hard stuff. Maybe it's how we handled losing our parents, it was a busy time, making arrangements and getting the house closed. We talked in spurts but never really to deal with it. Over the years, it has crept up in conversations, but we've never had a full on heart to heart. I think it was our way of keeping the hurt at bay. I agree with you, he needs to get it out, just not sure how you're going to get him sharing."

"Baby, I'm home," Alec announced walking in their house a little after 6:30pm.

He didn't hear Marren in the house, causing his heart to race. He walked through the house in a panic until he caught her reflection in the window of the sliding glass door.

Alec walked out on the patio, "What are you doing?"

"Planting the flowers Addison brought when she and the baby came over for lunch. He's so sweet. I offered to babysit this weekend if she and Max want to go out for dinner." Marren turned back to the flowers, "I hope the flowers grow a little before the wedding. I think they will look great in our pictures. What do you think?" Marren looked up to see Alec's panicked face. "What's going on?"

"I'll plant the flowers and take care of whatever you need in the backyard. You should be resting in the house. The alarm system wasn't on, you didn't answer when I called for you. What are you trying to do, give me a heart attack?"

Marren stood, brushing her hands off and speaking in a soft voice, "I'm trying to get back to normal. Dinner will be ready in ten minutes."

She walked to him, giving his waist a squeeze before walking through the sliding glass door into the kitchen.

"Marren, I want you safe."

Alec followed her, watching her wash her hands in the sink.

"You sound like you want me locked in the house and that's not going to happen," Marren said without a temper in her voice. She dried her hands, opening the oven and checking on their dinner.

"Using the security system isn't that big of an ask. Waiting for me to help with the yard work, not a big ask. Can't you just give yourself a break, relax and heal?" Alec kept his voice calm and gentle, even though an inferno was burning inside.

Using hot pads, Marren pulled the chicken out of the oven, placed it on the counter and closed the oven door.

"I am healing. Getting back to life is helping me heal. You should try it. I want us to be like we used to be. Talk to me, Alec. Make love to me. Hell, fight with me if you want but stop treating me like glass."

Alec stood before her, unsure what to say. Marren took a plate off the shelf and a set of silverware from the drawer, setting them next to the food, ready for dinner.

"I'm not hungry, I think I'll take a bath. I hope it's good," Marren said, walking out of the kitchen.

Alec called to her, "Marren." His voice was unsteady, "I'm not being unreasonable. I could have lost you."

"You didn't lose me. I didn't lose you. We have to stop acting like we did. We need to talk about what happened. You feel guilty and it shows in how you're treating me."

"Of course I feel guilty! The entire situation was my fault. He came after you because of me."

"No Alec, you're wrong. He came after me because of him. Martin took me in the daylight, in front of the precinct. I was parked four parking spaces from the entrance. I wasn't looking for him or anyone to hurt me because I was in a safe place. Who would be bold or crazy enough to do something like that? You cannot protect yourself against someone who is willing to exchange his or her life or freedom to hurt you. That person is crazy, how do you protect yourself against crazy?" Marren shook her head, "I've gone over it a million times, why didn't I see him approach? Why wasn't I looking for him? I felt safe and you're not to blame. Even if you walked me to my car, he would have followed me. Remember, I was going shopping. What you did after, every move you made is why I'm standing here with no permanent scars." Marren approached him, "Look at me." She took his hand, placing it on her cheek. Looking in his eyes she said, "You saved me. You did everything right." She turned her face, kissing the palm of his hand. "I'm going to take that bath."

Marren was hopeful Alec would join her in the bath but he didn't. With a towel wrapped around her body, she opened the bathroom door that joined to their bedroom, finding Alec sitting on the edge of the bed waiting for her.

"It's not just you I would have lost. Our future, our baby, he could have taken that away. I don't know how to live without you. My life won't make sense. You have to understand that I won't survive it, I won't. Seeing you, the way he…." Alec bowed his head, "knowing how scared you must have been." Alec's thoughts were spoken in fragments.

Marren stood between his legs, wrapping her arms around his shoulders.

"I thought of you. How much you love me, how I love you. That's what I thought of when I was scared. I played memories of us in a loop, that's what I held on to. Play those thoughts in your mind, stop concentrating on one night." Marren placed soft kisses down Alec's neck. "I love you," she whispered behind his ear.

Alec felt the warmth of Marren pressed against his body. His hands longed to touch her soft skin. For weeks he had held himself at bay, feeling he wasn't deserving of her since he couldn't stop the pain Martin inflicted. Marren's hands let go of him briefly to unbind the towel that sheltered her body, letting it fall before his feet.

Her breath returned to his neck commanding, "Please Alec, touch me. I need to feel you everywhere."

Alec hadn't realized he was holding his breath until Marren's hands touched his bare chest after she removed his shirt to press her breasts against him. His hands couldn't be still; they roamed over her, feeling her softness, grasping her breasts, tugging her ass cheeks to get her closer. His exhale was heard as a growl of need.

"Take me," Marren encouraged, "I'm yours. I need you."

Alec twisted Marren around, placing her on the bed. He stood before her to remove the rest of his clothes. Alec looked in her eyes, seeing the fire and want, the same feelings that he felt pulsing through his entire body.

"You are the most beautiful woman I have ever seen." He crawled over her, "I need you, baby."

His fingers slid over her center, feeling welcomed with heat and wetness. Alec wasted no time filling her with two fingers to ready her for him. He watched Marren's body arch to meet him.

"I love you, Marren. So fucking much."

Alec moved gently, sliding inside her. Marren's hands pulled his lower back, forcing him that much deeper.

"Slow, baby," Alec crooned.

Neither Alec nor Marren lasted any length of time before complete bliss took over. Marren moved to Alec's side when he rolled to his back. Every inch of her touched him with her signature cuddle. Alec's arm pulled her tight, his hand stroking her hair and face.

"You ok?" Alec asked.

"Better than ok." She tilted her face to look in his eyes, "I need you like this to feel beautiful, to feel whole. No part of you can leave me."

Alec's body turned to face her and his hand brushed her cheek, "I'm never leaving you. You have all of me. I'm sorry for…"

Marren's finger touched his lips to quiet him, "No more *sorry* about what happened to us. We have a wedding and a baby to get ready for. We love each other. We're moving forward."

Alec nodded, "Yes." His hand moved to her lower stomach as Marren rolled to her back. "My babies, you and this little one. What are you hoping for, a boy or girl?"

"Healthy." Marren responded with a grin, "I will be thrilled with a boy or a girl. Do you have a preference?"

"This time, because we're having lots more," Alec winked, "I think girl. Pretty little girl that looks like her mom."

"Lots more? Like how many are you thinking?" Marren giggled.

Alec moved his body between her legs, "As many as you let me put inside you." Alec rubbed his face back and forth across Marren's breasts.

"I was thinking two or three, but let's concentrate on this one first," Marren giggled again.

She stroked Alec's hair and sighed. They were back.

CHAPTER 22

Max gave Alec's shoulder a manly clasp, "Ready?"

"Ready? I've been waiting for this day for a long time." Alec checked his suit sleeves and buttons with nervous energy. "Did you check on Marren and Addison?"

Max nodded, "Sure did."

"Well?"

Before Max could respond, the music started, and all eyes turned to the French doors. The backyard was decorated exquisitely with a palette of ivory and white décor. A beautiful brick path led the way to the rose arch where Alec stood waiting for Marren. The colonel appeared in the door, lifting his elbow for Marren's hand. When she stepped from the house, her eyes immediately found Alec's. She was delighted to see the exact response she had hoped for. Alec's eyes were unable to blink. His hand touched his heart when he took a deep breath. Marren displayed the perfect smile. It was a smile that would be burnt in Alec's memory forever.

He mouthed, "So beautiful," with an infectious grin.

Marren smiled all the more.

Alec took Marren's hand and he couldn't help himself. He pulled her to him, kissing her gently.

His lips, still touching hers, moved saying, "I love you. You're gorgeous."

The minister cleared his throat, "Alec, it's not quite time for that."

Friends and family laughed quietly.

Vows were exchanged, readings were given by friends, candles were lit and finally, "You may kiss your bride, for the second time."

The couple grinned, wrapping their arms around each other. Alec kissed Marren thoroughly, receiving yelps and cheers from their guests.

When his mouth lifted, he sighed, "You, this life is everything I've ever wanted."

ADDITIONAL BOOKS BY ANSLEY PRESCOTT

Lean more:

www.ansleyprescott.com

Forever Fairhope Series:

Fairhope Ophelia

Fairhope Addison

Fairhope Paisley

Fairhope Jubileigh

Fairhope Marren

Fairhope Magnolia (Coming 2020)

Fairhope Delilah (Coming 2020)

Stand Alone Romance Books

Friends with Benefits